Evgeny
ZAMYATIN

We

Evgeny ZAMYATIN

We

A NOVEL

Moscow
Raduga Publishers
2000

ББК 84Р7—4
    326

Перевод *А. Миллера*
Художник *А. Никулин*

Замятин, Евгений

326   Мы: Роман. (на англ. яз.) М.: ОАО Изда-
        тельство «Радуга», 2000. — 256 с.

ISBN 5-05-004845-1   © English translation Raduga Pub-
                              lishers, 1991
                            © Design Raduga Publishers, 1999.

Entry No 1
Summary:

ANNOUNCEMENT. THE WISEST OF LINES. POEM.

I am simply copying out, word for word, what was published in today's State Newspaper:

"The construction of INTEGRAL will be completed in 120 days. The great and historic hour is nigh when the first INTEGRAL will soar into outer space. A thousand years ago, your heroic forbears subjected the whole terrestrial globe to the power of the Unified State. An even greater exploit now lies before you: to integrate the infinite equation of the Universe with glass, electric, fire-breathing INTEGRAL. To the beneficent yoke of reason you are going to subject unknown beings inhabiting other planets—perhaps still in a savage state of freedom. If they fail to understand that we are taking them mathematically infallible happiness, it will be our duty to force it upon them. But we shall try words before arms.

In the name of the Benefactor, it is hereby announced to all numbers in the Unified State that:

Each who feels capable must draw up tracts, poems, manifestoes, odes or other compositions about the beauty and majesty of the Unified State.

They will be the first cargo carried by INTEGRAL.

Long live the Unified State, long live the numbers, long live the Benefactor!"

I can feel my cheeks burning as I write this. Yes, to integrate the grandiose equation of the universe. Yes, to unbend the savage curve, to straighten it out as a tangent, an asymptote, into a straight line. Because the line of the Unified State is a straight line. A great, divine, precise, wise straight line, the wisest of all lines...

I, D-503, constructor of *Integral*, am only one of the mathematicians in the Unified State. My pen, accustomed to figures, hasn't the power to create the music of assonances and rhymes. I shall merely try to write down what I see and what I think—to be more precise, what we think (precisely so: we, and let that "WE" be the title of my notes). But this will, after all, be the product of our life, of the mathematically perfect life of the Unified State, and if so, then will it not, of itself, independently of my volition, be a poem? It will—this I believe and know.

As I write this, I feel my cheeks burning. It is probably similar to what a woman experiences when she first hears in her body the pulse of the new, still tiny, blind little human being. It is I and yet not I. And for many long months I shall have to feed it with my own life's blood and then tear it out of myself in pain and lay it at the feet of the Unified State.

But I am ready, as is each one, or almost each one of us. I am ready.

BALLET. SQUARE HARMONY. X.

Spring. From behind the Green Wall, from the wild, invisible plains, the wind is bearing the yellow honey-dust of flowers. Your lips go dry at this sweet dust—you lick them every few seconds—and perhaps all the women you meet have sweet lips (and the men too, of course). This is something of an obstacle to logical thought.

But the sky! Dark-blue, unsullied by a single cloud (what savage tastes the ancients had if their poets could be inspired by those clumsy, random heaps of steam jostling one another so fatuously up there). I love—I'm sure I won't be wrong if I say this: we love only that sterile, impeccable sky. On such days as this, the world is cast in the same stable, eternal glass as is the Green Wall, as are all our buildings. On such days you can see the dark-blue depths of things and their hitherto unknown and astounding equations—and you can see all this in what is altogether customary and everyday.

For instance. This morning I was at the ship-yard where *Integral* is being built, and suddenly I saw the machine-tools: with closed eyes, self-oblivious, the balls of the centrifugal governors were spinning round and round; shining crankshafts were bending to right and left; the beam was proudly shaking its shoulders; the chisel of a mortising machine was performing a Cossack dance in time to inaudible music. I suddenly saw all the beauty of this grandiose ballet of machines in the pale-blue rays of the sun.

And then I ask myself: why beautiful? Why is the dance beautiful? Answer: because it is a *non-free* movement, because all the profound meaning of the dance is precisely in absolute aesthetic sub-ordination, in ideal non-freedom. And if it is true that our forbears surrendered themselves to dancing at the most inspired moments of their life (religious mysteries, military parades), this can only mean one thing: the instinct of non-freedom has from ancient times been organically innate in man, and we, in our life today—only consciously...

I shall have to finish this later. The numerator has just clicked. I look up: 0-90, of course. Half a minute later, she will call on me in person for the promenade.

Dear O! It has always seemed to me that she is like her name: 10 centimetres below the Maternal Norm, so that she has been turned to round-ness in a lathe, and the pink O of her mouth is open to take in my every word. And, moreover, the circular, puffy fold round the wrist, such as you see on children.

When she came in, the logical flywheel was still humming inside me, and, out of inertia, I began talking about my newly established formula which covered all of us, and the machines, and the dance.

"It's wonderful, isn't it?" I asked.

"Yes, it's wonderful. Spring..." And 0-90 smiled rosily at me.

Oh, really—Spring, if you please... She was harping about spring. Women... I fell silent.

Down below. The prospekt is full. In such weather, we usually devote the after-dinner personal hour to an additional promenade. As always, the Music Factory was playing the March of the Unified State on all trumpets. In measured ranks, four abreast, extatically beating out the time, went the numbers—hundreds, thousands of numbers in pale-blue unifas[1] with gold plaques on their chests—the state number of each male and female. And I—we, the four of us—make up one of the countless waves in this mighty stream. On the left of me is 0-90 (if this was being written by one of my hairy ancestors some thousand years ago, he would doubtless qualify her with that ridiculous word "my"). On my right are two other unfamiliar numbers, one male, one female.

The blissfully dark-blue sky, the tiny children's suns in each of the plaques, and each sun unsullied by the madness of personal thoughts... Rays—you understand that everything comes from unified, radiant, smiling matter. And the brass rhythm: *"Tra-ta-tam. Tra-ta-ta-tam,"* those brass stairs glittering in the sun, and with each step you mount still higher, into the vertiginous blue...

And now, just as that morning at the shipyard,

---

[1] Probably from the ancient "uniform".

9

as if only now for the first time in my life, I saw everything: the unswerving straight streets, the glass of the road surfaces darting rays of light, the divine parallelepipeds of the transparent dwelling-houses, the square harmony of the grey-blue ranks on the march. As if it were not whole generations, but I, I alone had conquered the old God and the old life, I alone had created all this and I was like a tower, I was afraid to move my elbow lest I scatter the fragments of walls, domes, machines...

And then a split second, a jump across the ages from + to -. I remembered (evidently, association by contrast)—I suddenly remembered a picture in a museum: an avenue in their twentieth century, a deafeningly motley, confused crush of people, wheels, animals, notices, trees, colours, birds... And they say it really was like that then. It might have been. It seemed so unreal to me, so absurd, that I could not bear it and suddenly burst out laughing.

And promptly echoing laughter on my right. I turned my head and saw right in front of me the white, unusually white, sharp teeth and the face of a woman unfamiliar to me.

"I'm sorry," she said, "but you were looking round at everything with such inspiration, like a mythical god on the seventh day of creation. It seems to me you're certain that you, and no one else, also created me. I'm most flattered..."

All this without a smile, I would even say with a certain respectfulness (perhaps she knows that I am the constructor of *Integral*). But I don't know;

there was a strange, tantalising x in her eyes or her eyebrows, and I just couldn't catch it, I couldn't give it a numerical expression.

I felt embarrassed for some reason and, slightly muddle-headed, I began logically motivating my laughter. It was perfectly clear that this contrast, this impassable gulf between today and the past...

"But why impassable? (What white teeth!) You can throw a bridge over a gulf. Just imagine: a drum, battalions, ranks—such things happened too, and so that means..."

"But of course, it's clear!" she cried (it was a remarkable crossing of thoughts: in almost my own words, she had said what I had been jotting down before the promenade). "Even thoughts, you see. It's because no one is 'alone', each is 'one of'. We are identical..."

She:

"Are you sure?"

I saw the brows tilted up at an acute angle to the temples, like the sharp horns of x and for some reason I lost my bearings again, looked to the right, to the left, and...

She was on my right, slender, sharp, as firmly supple as a willow-wand—I-330 (I could now see her number). On my left was O, altogether different, all curves, with the child's fold on her wrist. And one of our four, a male number unfamiliar to me, double-curved like the letter S. We were all different...

She on my right, I-330, had evidently intercepted my distraught glance.

11

"Yes... Alas!" she said with a sigh.

In effect, that "Alas!" was entirely appropriate. But again there was something on her face or in her voice...

"Alas nothing," I said with a harshness unusual for me. "Science is advancing, and it's clear that if not now, then in fifty, a hundred years..."

"Even all our noses..."

"Yes, noses," I almost shouted. "Once it's there, it doesn't matter what the pretext is for envy... If I have a button-nose, but someone else..."

"Why, your nose is perhaps even 'Roman', as they used to say in ancient times. As for the hands... Come on, show me them, show me your hands!"

I can't bear it when people look at my hands. Covered in hair and shaggy, they're a sort of ugly atavism. I held them out. "Monkey's paws," I said, trying to sound detached.

She glanced at them, then at my face.

"But this is a very curious combination." She looked me over, as if I were on scales, and the horns at the corners of her eyebrows flickered again.

"He's registered for me," said 0-90, opening her joyously rosy mouth.

She should have kept quiet: it was completely off the point. Actually, that nice O—how am I to put it?—the speed of her tongue was incorrectly calculated; the velocity of tongue should always be a little less than the velocity of thought, never the other way round.

At the end of the prospekt, the bell was boom-

12

ing 17 on the accumulator tower. The personal hour was over. I-330 went away with the S-shaped male number. He had an impressive respectfulness and, as I now realised, what seemed to be a familiar face. I had met him before, but couldn't remember where at that particular moment.

In farewell, she smiled at me in the same x-fashion.

"Drop into auditorium one hundred and twelve the day after tomorrow."

I shrugged my shoulders.

"If I have a warrant for the auditorium you mentioned..."

"There will be one," she said with baffling certitude.

The woman had as unpleasant an effect on me as an indivisible irrational term that has fortuitously insinuated itself into an equation. I was glad to be left alone with my dear O, even if only for a short time.

We walked arm-in-arm across four lines of prospekts together. At the corner, she had to turn right, I had to turn left.

"I would so like to come to your place today and lower the blinds. This very day, right now..." said O, timidly looking up at me with her round, crystal-blue eyes.

She was so amusing. What could I say to her? She had been with me only the day before and knew as well as I did that our next day of sex was in two days' time. It was the same "thought an-

13

ticipation" that happens (sometimes destructively) when the ignition fires prematurely in an engine.

As we parted, I kissed her two ... no, I'll be more precise, three times, those wonderful, dark-blue, unclouded eyes of hers.

Entry No. 3
Summary:

JACKET. WALL. TABLET.

I've run through everything I wrote yesterday and I can see that I didn't write clearly enough. That is, it's all perfectly clear to any of us. But how am I to know? Perhaps you, the unknown ones, to whom *Integral* will take my notes, have read the great book of civilisation only as far as the page that our ancestors reached 900 years ago. Perhaps you do not even know such rudiments as the Tablet of Hours, the Personal Hours, the Maternal Norm, the Green Wall, or the Benefactor. I find it amusing and yet very difficult to talk about all this. It is, indeed, just as if a writer of, say, the 20th century had to give explanations in his novel of "jacket, "flat" or "wife". Incidentally, if his novel is translated for savages, is it conceivable that there should be no notes on "jacket"?

I am sure that the savage looked at the "jacket" and thought, "What's that for? Just a burden." It seems to me that you will look in just the same way when I tell you that none of us has been behind the Green Wall since the times of the Two Hundred Years War.

But, my dear friends, you must do a little thinking, it is a great help. After all, the whole of human history, as we know it, is clearly the history of the transition from nomadic to more settled forms of life. Does it not follow from this that the most settled form of life (our own) is also the most perfect (our own)? If people once drifted over the Earth from end to end, it was only in prehistoric times, when there were nations, wars, trade and the discovery of various Americas. But who needs all that now, and to what end?

I grant that becoming accustomed to this settled life was not achieved without difficulty, and not overnight. When, during the Two Hundred Years War, all the roads were destroyed and were overgrown with grass, it must initially have seemed very uncomfortable for people to live in cities, cut off from one another by green forests. But what came from this? After man's tail dropped off, it probably took him some time to learn to chase the flies away without the use of a tail. At first, he must surely have been miserable without it. But now—can you imagine yourself with a tail? Or can you imagine yourself naked on the street, without a "jacket" (you may still be strolling about in "jackets"). That's how it is here: I cannot imagine a city not dressed in a Green Wall, I cannot imagine life not arrayed in the digital vestments of the Tablet.

The Tablet... At this very moment, its purple

digits on their gold background are looking tenderly and sternly at me from the wall in my room. I involuntarily recall what the ancients called an "icon", and I want to compose poetry or prayers (they are the same thing). Oh, why am I not a poet that I might worthily extol you, O Tablet, O heart and pulse of the Unified State?

While still at school, all of us (and maybe you too) read that most majestic of all the ancient literary monuments that have come down to us, the *Railway Timetable*. But if you put even that side by side with the Tablet, you will see graphite next to a diamond: both consist of the same thing, carbon, but how eternal, how translucent is the glittering diamond. Who will not catch his breath when thundering at speed through the pages of the *Timetable*? But the Tablet of the Hours turns each of us in real life into the steel, six-wheeled hero of the great poem. Every morning, with six-wheeled precision, at exactly the same hour and exactly the same minute, millions of us rise as one. At exactly the same hour, we, in our unified millions, start work and in our unified millions we finish it. And, merging into the single, million-handed body at exactly the second appointed by the Tablet, we raise our spoons to our mouths and at exactly the same second we go out for a promenade and proceed into the auditorium, into the hall of the Taylor Exercises, and in the same wise we retire to bed...

I will be completely frank: we have not found an absolutely precise solution for the problem of happiness either. From 16 to 17 and from 21 to 22, the unified powerful organism breaks up into separate cells: these are the Personal Hours fixed by the Tablet. During these hours, some have their blinds discreetly lowered, others are proceeding along the prospekt to the brass tempo of the March, others, as I am now, are at their desks. But I firmly believe, and let me be called an idealist and a dreamer for doing so, I believe that sooner or later, but eventually for these hours too, we shall find a place in the general formula; all 86,400 seconds will ultimately go into the Tablet of the Hours.

I have read and heard many unpleasant things about the times when people still lived in a free, i.e. disorganised and savage state. But what has always seemed incredible to me is how the state power of that time, even when embryonic, could allow people to live without anything even resembling our Tablet, without compulsory promenades, without precisely regulated mealtimes, and to get up and go to bed whenever they felt like it. Some historians even say that in those times the lights burned in the streets and people walked and rode about all through the night.

That is something of which I simply cannot make sense. After all, however limited their powers of reason may have been, they must surely have understood that such a life was nothing less than mass murder, but carried out slowly, day by day. The state (humaneness) forbade the murder of an individual, but did not forbid the half-murder of millions. It was a crime to kill one person, i.e. to

17

reduce the total of human lives by 50 years, but it was not a crime to reduce the sum total of human lives by 50 million years. Is that not ridiculous? Here, any ten-year-old will solve that mathematically moral problem in half a minute. But they couldn't: not all their Kants taken together (because not one of those Kants ever thought of constructing a system of scientific ethics, i.e. ethics founded on subtraction, addition, division and multiplication).

And is it not absurd that the state (it had the nerve to call itself a state!) was able to leave sexual life without any control whatever? Whoever wanted it, and at will. Unscientifically, like beasts. And, like beasts, blindly, they procreated. Is it not ridiculous: to know gardening, chicken-farming, fish-farming (we have exact data to show that they knew all these things) and not to be able to step up on to the last rung of this logical ladder: child-farming? Not to proceed logically to our Maternal and Paternal Norms?

It's so ludicrous, so unlikely that I should have written this and be afraid: what if you, my unknown readers, suddenly take me for an evil joker? And suddenly think that I simply want to make fun of you and am talking utter drivel with a solemn face?

But, first, I'm not capable of jokes: falsehood goes into every joke as an implicit function; secondly, the Unified State Science affirms that the life of the ancients was exactly like that, and the Unified State Science cannot err. Indeed, where was it possible to obtain state logic in those times when people lived in a condition of freedom, in other words, the condition of beasts, apes, the herd? What could be demanded of them if, even in our own time, it is still possible to hear now and then, a wild, apelike echo from somewhere down below, from the shaggy depths? Fortunately, only now and then.

Fortunately, these are only minor breakdowns of the components; they can easily be repaired without stopping the eternal, great running of the whole Machine. And to cast out the bent bolt, we have the skilful, heavy hand of the Benefactor, we have the experienced eyes of the Guardians...

Yes, and by the way, I've just remembered: that man yesterday, double-curved like an S—I think I've seen him several times coming out of the Guardians' Bureau. Now I know why I had an instinctive feeling of respect for him and a kind of embarrassment when, in his presence, that strange I-330... I must admit that she...

Bedtime's ringing: 22.30. Until tomorrow.

Entry No. 4
Summary:

THE SAVAGE
WITH THE BAROMETER.
EPILEPSY. IF ONLY.

Until now, everything in life has been clear to me (it's not for nothing, I think, that I have a certain partiality for the word "clear"). But today... I don't understand.

19

First, I have indeed received a warrant for Auditorium No. 112, just as she told me. Although the probability was $\frac{1,500}{10,000,000} = \frac{3}{20,000}$ (1,500 being the number of auditoriums and 10,000,000 the total of human numbers). Secondly... But it would be better to stick to the sequence of events.

The auditorium. An enormous hemisphere of glass blocks with the sun streaming right through it. Circular rows of nobly spheroid, smoothly shaven heads. I looked round me and my heart sank faintly. I think I was looking for something: wouldn't the rosy sickle of O's dear lips shine somewhere over the pale blue waves of the unifas? Yonder I could see uncommonly white, sharp teeth, like... No, I was mistaken. This evening, at 21, O would come to me: the desire to see her here was perfectly natural.

The bell rang. We stood up and sang the Anthem of the Unified State. On the stage, the phonolector sparkled with a gold loudspeaker and wit.

"Respected Numbers! Archaeologists recently unearthed a book of the twentieth century. In it, the author speaks ironically of a savage and a barometer. The savage noticed that every time the barometer stopped on "Rain", it did indeed rain. And since the savage wanted rain, he extracted just enough mercury for the level to stop at "Rain" (on the screen, a savage in feathers pulling out mercury. Laughter.). You are laughing. But doesn't it seem to you that far more deserving of laughter is the European of that era. Just like the savage, the European wanted rain, rain with a capital "r", algebraic rain. But he stood in front of the barometer like a wet hen. At least the savage had more boldness and energy and—although savage—he still had logic. He was able to establish that there is a connection between cause and effect. By picking out the mercury, he was able to take the first step forward along the great road over which..."

At this point (I repeat that I write without hiding anything), I became temporarily impervious to the lifegiving currents pouring from the loudspeakers. It suddenly seemed to me that I had come here in vain (why "in vain" and how could I not have come, since I had been given a warrant?). It seemed to me that everything was trivial, just a shell. I only switched on my attention with an effort when the phonolector went over to the main theme: our music, mathematical composition (mathematician as cause, music as effect), a description of the recently invented musicometer.

"Simply by turning this handle, any one of you can churn out up to three sonatas an hour. And what a sweat it was for your ancestors! They could only create by driving themselves to fits of 'inspiration', an unknown form of epilepsy. And here is a highly amusing illustration of what they got out of it—the músic of Scriabin—the twentieth century. This black box (curtains were opened on the stage and there was their most ancient instrument)—this box was called a 'grand', which proves yet again how far all their music..."

And so on. I've forgotten again, most likely because... Well, I'll put it straight: because she, I—330, went up to the "grand" box. I was probably just shaken by her unexpected appearance on the stage.

She was wearing the fantastic attire of ancient times: a clinging black dress, the sharply outlined white of the bare shoulders and chest, and, as she breathed, that warm shadow quivering between... And those dazzling, almost vicious teeth...

Her smile was a bite-down to the audience. She took her seat and began playing. Wild, convulsive, multicoloured, like the whole of their life in those days. And, of course, those around me were right: they were all laughing. Only a few ... but why I too—I?

Yes, epilepsy, a mental disease, pain... Slow, sweet pain—a bite—and let it be deeper and still more painful. And now, slowly, the sun. Not our own sun, not that pale-blue crystal and even sun that shines through the glass bricks—no. A wild, onward-rushing, blasting sun—take everything off, tear everything to shreds.

The man sitting on my right glanced at me and sniggered. I remember it very distinctly, for some reason. I saw a microscopic bubble of saliva start up on his lips and burst. That bubble sobered me down. I was myself again. Like all the others, I could hear nothing but an absurd, busy-busy jangling of strings. I was laughing. Everything became easy and simple. The talented phonolector had pictured that savage era too vividly for us, and that's all there was to it.

With what pleasure I listened afterwards to the music of our own times. (It was demonstrated at the end for contrast.) Crystalline chromatic steps of infinite series converging and diverging—and the summarising chords of Taylor and Maclaurin formulae; full-tone, square-loaded moves of Pythagoras' trousers; the sad melodies of dying vibrato movement; vivid beats alternating with Fraunhofer lines of pauses—the spectral analysis of the planets... What majesty! What unshakeable inevitability! And how pathetic it was, the self-willed music of the ancients that could offer nothing but wild fantasies.

As usual, all went out of the auditorium through the wide doors four abreast in an orderly manner. I had a glimpse of the familiar S-shaped figure. I bowed respectfully.

My dear O was due to arrive in an hour. I felt agreeably and usefully agitated. When I entered the house, I went to the office straightaway, thrust my rose ticket at the duty officer and collected my certificate for the right to lower my blinds. We only have this right on sex days. Otherwise, within our transparent walls which look as though they had been woven out of shining air, we always live on view, everlastingly bathed in light. We have nothing to hide from one another. Moreover, this eases the heavy and lofty labour of the Guardians. Otherwise, anything could happen. Perhaps it was the very strange, opaque dwellings of the ancients that engendered their pathetic cell mentality. "My (sic!) home is my castle"—how absurd!

At 21 I lowered the blinds, and at that precise moment O came in, slightly out of breath. She offered me a rosy little mouth and a rose ticket. I tore off the coupon, but could not tear myself away from the rosy mouth until the very last moment—22.15.

Then I showed her my diary "entries" and spoke—very well, apparently—about the beauty of the square, the cube and the straight line. She listened with such rosy charm, but suddenly a tear, then another, then a third fell from the blue eyes on to the open page (p.7). The ink was smudged. Oh well, I would have to write it out again.

"Dear D, if only you, if only..."

What was this "if only"? What did she mean by "if only"? Her old song again: a child. Or perhaps something new concerning ... concerning the other woman? Although here it was as if... No, that would be too absurd.

Entry No. 5
Summary:

THE SQUARE. THE MASTERS OF THE WORLD. AN AGREEABLY USEFUL FUNCTION.

Wrong again. I'm talking to you, again, my unknown reader, as if you were... Well, let's say, my old comrade, R-13, a poet with negroid lips—but then everybody knows him. Meanwhile you, on

24

the Moon, on Venus, on Mars, on Mercury—who knows where and who you are?

Here's what: imagine a square, a living, beautiful square. And you have to tell it about yourself and your life. You understand, it would never even enter a square's head to say how all its four angles are equal: it simply just doesn't see this, since, to it, this is very much a customary and everyday matter. Well, I'm in the same position as the square. Rose coupons and everything associated with them are, as far as I'm concerned, the equality of the four angles, but to you, all this may be even more complicated than Newton's binomial theorem.

So here we are. One of the ancient sages—by chance, needless to say—said a clever thing: "Love and starvation master the world." Ergo: in order to master the world, man must master the masters of the world. Our ancestors finally conquered Starvation, but they paid dearly for it. I'm referring to the Great Two Hundred Years War, the war between city and country. Probably because of their religious prejudices, the savage Christians held stubbornly on to their "bread"[1]. But in the year '35—before the foundation of the Unified State—our present oil food was invented. True, only 0.2 of the world's population survived. However, purified of a thousand years' filth, how radi-

[1] This word has survived amongst us solely as a poetic metaphor. The chemical composition of the substance is not known to us.

ant the face of the Earth became! Even so, those zero point two tasted bliss in the chambers of the Unified State.

Is it not clear that bliss and envy are the numerator and denominator of the fraction called happiness? And what would have been the point of all the countless victims in the Two Hundred Years War if there still remained a cause for envy in our life? But it has remained, because people with "button" and Roman noses are still with us (our conversation during the promenade), because many sought the love of some, but no one sought that of the others.

It is natural that the Unified State, in subjecting Famine to itself (algebraic = the sum of external benefits), led an offensive against the other master of the world, love. Finally this elemental force too was defeated, i.e. organised and mathematicised, and about 300 years ago our historic "Lex sexualis" was proclaimed: "Each of the numbers has the right to any other number as a sex product."

Well, the rest is technology. You are being meticulously studied in the laboratories of the Sex Bureau, where they determine the exact content of sex hormones in the blood and work out the corresponding Table of sex days for you. Then you make an application stating that on your days you wish to use such-and-such a number and you are issued with the appropriate coupon book (pink). That's all there is to it.

It's all clear: there are no more causes whatever

for jealousy, the numerator of the happiness fraction has been reduced to zero and the fraction has been converted into magnificent infinity. The very thing that was a source of countless extremely stupid tragedies for the ancients, has led, in our society, to a harmonious, agreeably useful function of the organism like sleep, physical labour, the ingestion of food, defecation, and so on. From this you can see how the great power of logic purifies everything it touches. Oh, if only you, the unknown ones, could have this divine power, if only you too could learn to follow it to the end.

...It's strange, but I was writing today of the supreme heights in human history, and I was breathing the purest mountain air of thought all the time; but I was all cloudy and cobwebby inside, and it was as if there was a kind of four-pawed x in me, like a cross. Or they are my paws, and all because they've been before my eyes for a long time, those hairy paws of mine? I hate talking about them, and I hate them: they are a throwback to the savage era. Could it be that there really is in me— —

I wanted to delete all this because it is outside the range of the summary. But then I decided not to delete it after all. Let my entries, like a highly sensitive seismograph, plot the curve of even the most insignificant cerebral oscillations. After all, these are precisely the oscillations that sometimes serve as a portent—

But this is already an absurdity and it really ought to be deleted: all the elements have been channelled by us and there cannot be any catastrophes.

It is now perfectly clear to me that this strange feeling inside me all comes from my square position, which I already mentioned at the beginning. And it's not the x in me (that is impossible), it's simply that I am afraid of some kind of x being left in you, my unknown readers. But I believe you will not judge me too harshly. I believe you will understand that it is harder for me to write than ever it was for many a writer throughout the whole of human history; some wrote for their contemporaries, others for posterity, but not one of them ever wrote for his ancestors or for creatures similar to his savage, remote ancestors...

Entry No. 6
Summary:

CHANCE. THE ACCURSED "IT'S CLEAR". 24 HOURS.

I repeat: I have imposed on myself the obligation to write without concealing anything. Consequently, however sad this may be, I must note here that, even with us, the hardening, the crystallisation of life is evidently not yet over; there are still a few more stages before the ideal. The ideal (as is clear) is where nothing happens any more, but with us... Take this, if you please. I read today in the State Newspaper that in two days' time there will be a Festival of Justice. This means that one of the numbers has disrupted the movement of the State Machine and something unforeseen and incalculable has happened again.

Moreover, something has happened to me. True, it was during the Personal Hour, i.e. the time specially put aside for unforeseen circumstances, but even so...

At about 16 (to be precise, at ten to 16) I was at home. Suddenly, the telephone rang.

"D-503?" A woman's voice.

"Yes."

"Are you free?"

"Yes."

"This is me, I-330. I'm going to drop in and pick you up now. We'll leave for the Ancient House. Agreed?"

I-330... She irritates, repels, almost frightens me. But for that very reason I said, "Yes."

Within 5 minutes we were already aboard the aero. Dark-blue May majolica of the sky; the light sun on its own golden aero buzzing behind us, neither overtaking us nor falling behind. But far in front of us was the white blob of a cloud, grotesque, inflated, like the cheeks of an ancient "Cupid", and this hindered me somehow. The front window was raised, there was a wind, my lips dried, I had to keep licking them and thinking about lips all the time.

And now some blurred green blobs were visible ahead of us on the far side of the Wall. Then a light, sinking sensation in the pit of the stomach—down, down, down, as from the top of a steep mountain, and here we were at the Ancient House.

The whole of that strange, fragile building was clad in a glass shell: otherwise, it would, of course, have collapsed long ago. At the glass door stood an old woman, all wrinkles, especially her mouth: nothing but creases and puckers; her lips had already curved inwards, her mouth had somehow become covered with skin and it seemed absolutely incredible that she should start talking. But that was exactly what she did. "Well, dearies, have you come to have a look at my little house?"

And her wrinkles radiated outwards (i. e. probably assumed the form of rays, which created the impression that they "radiated").

"Yes, grannie, I want to see it again," said I-330.

The wrinkles beamed.

"The sun today, eh? Well, what d'you want? Oh, you naughty girl, oh, you naughty girl! I know, I know! Very well, then, go in on your own, I'd better stay out here in the sun..."

Hm... My companion was probably a frequent visitor to this place. I wanted to brush something off myself—it was bothering me. Perhaps it was still that persistent visual image: the cloud on the smooth, dark-blue majolica.

While we were climbing the broad, dark staircase, she said.

"I love her, that old woman."

"Why?"

"I don't know. Perhaps because of her mouth. Or perhaps for no particular reason I simply love her."

I shrugged my shoulders. Smiling faintly, or perhaps not even smiling at all, she continued.

"I feel very guilty. Clearly, there shouldn't be 'just-simple-love', there should be 'because-it's-love'. All elements should be..."

"It's clear ... I began, but promptly pulled myself up short on the word and glanced at her furtively. Had she noticed?

She was looking somewhere downwards: her eyes were lowered, like blinds. I remembered something in the evenings: at about 22, I was walking along the prospekt and amid the brilliantly illuminated transparent cells there were some dark ones with lowered blinds, and there, behind those blinds— — What was going on behind her own blinds? Why did she ring up today, and what was all this about?

I opened a heavy, creaking, opaque door and we were in a gloomy, untidy apartment (they used to call it a "flat"). That same strange "grand" musical instrument, and a savage, disorganized medley of colours and forms, like the music of those times. A white surface overhead, dark-blue walls, the red, green and orange bindings of ancient volumes, the yellow bronze of chandeliers and a statue of the Buddha, epileptically distorted lines of furniture that would never fit into any kind of equation.

31

I found this chaos hard to bear. But my companion was evidently made of sterner stuff.

"This is my favourite..." And suddenly she seemed to get a grip on herself: a biting smile, sharp white teeth. "To be precise, the most ugly of all their 'flats'."

"Or, to be even more precise, sovereign states," I corrected. "Thousands of microscopic, eternally warring sovereign states, as merciless as..."

"Well, yes, that's clear," she said, apparently with utter solemnity.

We went through a room in which stood tiny children's cots (children also were private property in that era). Then more rooms, the gleam of mirrors, gloomy cupboards, garishly coloured divans, an enormous "fireplace", a big bed of red wood. Our present-day glass, beautiful, transparent and everlasting, was only to be seen in the form of pathetically small and fragile window-squares.

"Just to think that here they 'simply loved', burned, suffered... (Again the lowered blinds of the eyes.) What a stupid, prodigal waste of human energy, isn't that so?"

She was speaking out of me, she was expressing my own thoughts. But there was still that irritating x in her smile. Behind those blinds, something, I don't know what, had been happening in her and it taxed my patience sorely. I wanted to argue with her, shout at her (yes, shout), but I had to agree, it was impossible to do otherwise.

We stopped in front of a mirror. At that moment, I could only see her eyes. I had an idea.

After all, man is arranged as absurdly as those ugly "flats"; human heads are opaque, and there are only tiny windows inside: the eyes. She guessed my thought somehow and turned to me. "All right, here are my eyes. Well?" (This was, of course, unspoken.)

In front of me were two eerily dark windows, and such an unknown, alien life inside. I could only see a fire: some kind of "fireplace" was ablaze in there, and I saw some figures that looked like...

This was natural, of course. I had caught sight of my own reflection. But it was unnatural and unlike me (evidently, the depressing effect of the surroundings), and I distinctly felt as if I had been caught and transplanted into that savage cell, as if I had been snatched up into the wild whirlwind of the ancient life.

"You know what," she said, "come into the next room for a moment." I could hear her voice from there, from inside, from behind the dark eye-windows in which the fire was blazing.

I went out and sat down. The snub-nosed, asymmetrical face of one of the ancient poets (Pushkin, apparently) was smiling almost imperceptibly straight at me from a small shelf on the wall. Why was I sitting like this, humbly submitting to that smile, and what was it all about? What was I doing here, and why was I in this stupid state of mind? This irritating, repulsive woman, this strange game...

The wardrobe door banged, silk rustled, and I

had to force myself not to go over there and—I don't remember exactly—I probably wanted to say some very harsh things to her.

But she had already come out. She was wearing a short, ancient bright-yellow dress, a black hat and black stockings. The dress was of thin silk, as I could clearly see. The stockings were very long, well above the knee, and the open neck, the shadow between...

"Listen, you obviously want to show how original you are, but do you really..."

"It's clear," she interrupted. "To be original means to stand out amongst the others. Consequently, to be original is to violate equality... And what in the idiotic language of the ancients was called 'being banal', means, to us, simply to do one's duty. Because..."

"Yes, yes, yes! Precisely." I couldn't contain myself. "And there's no point, no point at all in your..."

She went up to the statue of the snub-nosed poet and, pulling the blind down over the wild fire of her eyes, there, inside, behind her windows, apparently in all seriousness (perhaps to mollify me), she said a very reasonable thing this time:

"Don't you find it amazing that people once put up with his kind? Not only put up with them, but worshipped them. What a slavish spirit! Isn't that so?"

"It's clear... That is, I wanted... (That confounded 'It's clear'!)"

"Yes, I understand. But these were masters

stronger than their crowned ones. Why didn't they isolate them, why didn't they destroy them? In our time..."

"Yes, in our time..." I began. And suddenly she burst out laughing. I could see her laughter with my own eyes: the ringing, steep, supple resilient curve of that laughter, like a whiplash.

I remember trembling all over. I wanted to seize hold of her, and then—I don't remember exactly... I had to do something, never mind what. I automatically opened my gold plaque and glanced at my watch. It was ten to 17.

"Don't you find that our time is up?" I asked as politely as I could.

"And supposing I asked you to stay here with me?"

"Listen, do you ... do you know what you're saying? I have to be in the auditorium in ten minutes..."

"...And all numbers are obliged to undergo a set course of art and science..." she said in my voice. Then she pulled up the blind and raised her eyes: through the dark windows, I could see a fireplace blazing. "I have a doctor in the Medical Bureau: he's registered to me. If I ask him, he'll give you a certificate to say you were ill. Well?"

I understood. At last I understood what this game was all about.

"So that's how it is! But you know that like every honest number, I must, in fact, immediately go to the Guardians' Bureau and..."

"But not in actual fact (a sharp, biting smile).

35

I'm terribly curious. Will you or won't you go to the Bureau?"

"You're staying?" I took hold of the door-handle. It was made of brass and I could hear the same brass in my voice. "One moment... May I?"

She went to the telephone, called a number—I was too upset to memorise it—and shouted:

"I shall be waiting for you in the Ancient House. Yes, yes, on my own..."

I turned the cold brass door-handle.

"Will you permit me to take the aero?"

"Oh, yes, of course! Please do..."

The old woman was dozing in the sun outside at the entrance like a plant. It was again amazing to see her lips, so tightly grown together, suddenly open for her to say:

"That girl of yours—what's happened? Is she staying behind on her own?"

"Yes."

The old woman's lips grew together again. She shook her head. Even her failing mind understood all the stupidity and risk of that I-330's behaviour.

I was at the lecture at 17 on the dot. Then I suddenly remembered, for some reason, that I had told the old woman a lie. I-330 was not alone there now. Perhaps it was my unintentional deception of the old woman that was tormenting me so much and preventing me from listening to the lecture. No, I-330 wasn't alone: that was the whole point.

I had a free hour after 21.30. I could still go to the Guardians' Bureau and make a statement.

But I was so tired after the whole silly business. And anyway, the legal time for a statement is forty-eight hours. I would have time tomorrow, another full 24 hours.

Entry No. 7
Summary:

THE EYELASH. TAYLOR.
HENBANE AND LILIES-OF-THE-VALLEY.

Night. Green, orange, dark-blue; the red grand piano; the dress, yellow as an orange. Then, the brass Buddha; he suddenly raised his copper eyelids and juice flowed: out of the Buddha. And out of the yellow dress—juice, and drops of juice over the mirror, and the big bed is dripping, and the children's cots, and now so am I—and a kind of deadly-sweet horror...

I woke up. A moderate, bluish light. The glass of the walls was shining, the glass armchairs, the table. This calmed me a little and my heart stopped pounding. Juice, Buddha... What was the meaning of this absurdity? Obviously, I was ill. I had never had dreams before. They say that dreaming was quite ordinary and normal with the ancients. But of course: their whole life was just such an appalling merry-go-round: green, orange, Buddha, juice. As for us, we know that dreaming

37

is a serious psychic illness. And I know that hitherto my brain has a chronometrically adjusted glittering mechanism, without a single speck of dust anywhere. But now... Yes, now it's different: I can feel some kind of foreign body in my brain, like a very thin eyelash in the eye; I can feel my whole self, but this eye with the hair in it can't be forgotten for a moment...

A brisk, crystal little bell ringing at the head of my bed: 7, it's time to get up. To the right and left through the glass walls I can see myself, my room, my clothes and my movements all repeated a thousand times. This keeps my spirits up. I can see myself as part of one enormous, powerful, unified whole. And such precise beauty: not a single superfluous gesture, bend, or turn.

Yes, that Taylor was undoubtedly the greatest genius among the ancients. True, he didn't get as far as spreading his method to the whole of life, to each step, to twenty-four-hour periods; he could not integrate his system from one hour to twenty-four. But how could they write whole libraries about, say, Kant, and hardly take any notice of Taylor, that prophet who had been ten centuries ahead of his time?

Breakfast is over. The National Anthem of the Unified State has been sung. Harmoniously, in fours, to the lifts. The scarcely audible buzzing of the motors. And swiftly down, down, down—a light sinking sensation in the pit of the stomach.

And then suddenly that stupid dream again, or a kind of implicit function of it. Ah, yes, of course. It was the same on the aero yesterday: a steep descent. All that's over, however. Period. It's a good thing I was so firm and harsh with her.

I travelled in the underground carriage towards where the still inert, elegant hull of *Integral*, as yet uninspired by fire, was glittering in the shipyard under the sun. I closed my eyes and dreamed in formulae, still mentally calculating what initial velocity was necessary to tear *Integral* away from the Earth. Each atom of a second, the mass of *Integral* changes (the explosive fuel is being consumed). The resulting equation was very complicated, with transcendental magnitudes.

As if in a waking dream, there, in the solid world of numerical figures, someone sat beside me, nudged me lightly and said "Excuse me".

I half-opened my eyes and my first (association from *Integral*) impression was of something flying into space: a head, and it was flying because there were the protruding pink wings of ears at the sides. Then the curved line of the over-hanging nape of a neck, and a hunched back, an S bend.

And through the glass walls of my algebraic world, an eyelash, something unpleasant that I must do today—

"It's all right, it's all right, please," I said, smiling at my neighbour and bowing my head in greeting. He had S-4711 glittering on his plaque (now I could understand why I associated him with the letter S: it was a visual impression that had not registered itself on my consciousness). And the eyes flashed, two sharp gimlets spinning rapidly deeper and deeper, and at any moment now they would screw down to the very bottom and would see what even I myself...

Suddenly, the eyelash became perfectly clear to me: this was one of *them*, one of the Guardians, and it would be simplest of all to tell him everything straightaway without postponing it any longer...

"I was in the Ancient House yesterday, you know..." My voice was strange, squashed and flat. I tried to clear my throat.

"Excellent. That gives material for very instructive conclusions."

"But I wasn't alone, you understand; I was escorting Number I-330, and then..."

"I-330? I am happy for you. A very interesting and talented woman. She has many admirers."

...But he too—he had been on the promenade at the time, and, perhaps, he was even allocated to her. No, it was out of the question, it was unthinkable to talk to him about it, that was clear.

"Yes, yes! Certainly, certainly... A great many. I was smiling more and more broadly and stupidly; I felt that my smile was making me look naked and foolish...

The gimlets went down to the bottom of me, then, rotating rapidly, unscrewed themselves back up into his eyes. S gave me a double smile, nodded and slithered to the exit.

I hid behind my newspaper (I imagined everybody was staring at me) and soon forgot about the eyelash, the gimlets and everything else; I was too

40

disturbed by what I had read. One short line: According to reliable information, traces have again been discovered of the hitherto elusive organisation whose goal is liberation from the beneficial yoke of the State.

"Liberation"? Amazing how persistent were the criminal instincts in the human race. I say "criminal" with reason. Freedom and crime are as inseparably bound up with one another as... well, as the movement of an aero with its speed. If the speed of an aero = 0, it does not move; if the freedom of a man = 0, he doesn't commit any crimes. Clearly the only way to prevent a man from committing crimes is to deprive him of his freedom. We have only just rid ourselves of this (in the cosmic scale of a century, this, of course, is "only just") when suddenly certain pathetic dimwits... No, I don't understand. Why didn't I go at once to the Guardians' Bureau yesterday? I shall certainly call there after 16.

I came out at 16. 10 and immediately saw O on the corner, all rosy with delight at meeting me. "Now that one has a simple circular mind. That's convenient: she'll understand and back me up..." But no, I had no need of support: I had firmly made up my mind.

The trumpets of the Music Factory were harmoniously thundering out the March, that same daily March again. What indescribable charm in that dailiness, that repetitiveness, that mirrorness! O seized me by the hand.

"Let's go on the promenade." The round blue

eyes were wide open as they looked at me; they were dark-blue windows into the interior, and I went inside, getting caught in nothing: there was nothing there, i.e. nothing extraneous or unnecessary.

"No, not this time. I must go..." I told her where. And, to my amazement, the rosy circle of the mouth formed into a rosy crescent with the horns pointing downwards, as if she had tasted something sour. I blew up.

"You female numbers seem to be incurably consumed by prejudice. You are completely incapable of abstract thought. Excuse me, but that is sheer stupidity."

"You're going to the spies... Ugh! But it so happens that I got you a bunch of lilies-of-the-valley in the Botanic Museum..."

"Why 'But'? Why that 'But'? Just like a woman." Angrily (as I must admit), I snatched her lilies from her. "So here they are, your lilies-of-the-valley, all right? Have a sniff. Nice, aren't they? So have at least just this much logic. The lilies smell nice. Well and good. But can you say of the smell, of the very concept 'smell', that it is good or bad? You can't, eh? There is the scent of the lily, and there is the foul smell of henbane: each of them is a smell. There were spies in the ancient state, and we have spies too ... yes, spies: I'm not afraid of words. But it's clear that in those days, spies were henbane, whereas now they're lilies. Yes, lilies, that's what they are!"

The rosy crescent was quivering. I now realise that it only seemed so to me, but at the time I was convinced that she would laugh. And I shouted even louder:

"Yes, lilies! And there's nothing funny about it, nothing funny at all!"

The smooth, round globes of heads were floating past and turning round. O took me affectionately by the hand.

"Today you're sort of... You're not ill, are you?"

Dream—yellow—Buddha... It promptly became clear to me that I must go to the Medical Bureau.

"Yes, I really am ill after all," I said very happily (there was an inexplicable contradiction here: I had nothing to feel happy about).

"You must go to the doctor at once. After all, you understand yourself that it's your duty to be fit—it's ridiculous having to prove this to you."

"Well, my dear O, but of course, you're right. Absolutely right!"

I didn't go to the Guardians' Bureau. I had no choice but to go to the Medical Bureau instead. I was delayed there until 17.

In the evening (incidentally, it didn't matter in the evening, since they were already closed there), O came to visit me. We didn't lower the blinds. We decided to solve problems from an old book of maths problems. This calms and purifies the thoughts wonderfully well. With her head bent towards her left shoulder, O-90 sat over her exercise-book, pushing her tongue into her left cheek; she was trying so hard. It was so childlike and so charming. I felt all good, exact, and simple inside...

She left. I was alone. I sighed deeply twice (this is very useful before sleep). Suddenly there was an unforeseen scent—a hint of something very unpleasant... I soon found it. A spray of lilies-of-the-valley had been hidden in my bed. At once, everything was churned up and rose from the bottom. No, it was sheer tactlessness on her part, foisting those lilies on me. All right, I hadn't gone on the promenade after all. But it was hardly my fault if I was ill.

Entry No. 8
Summary:

THE IRRATIONAL SQUARE ROOT.
R-13. TRIANGLE.

It's such a long time ago since $\sqrt{-1}$ happened to me when I was at school. I remember it so clearly, so distinctly: the bright sphere of a hall, hundreds of little boys' round heads, and Plyapa, our mathematician. We had nicknamed him Plyapa because he was conspicuously ramshackle and loose at the joints by now, and when the duty man pushed a plug into him from behind, the loudspeaker always started off with "Plya-plya-plya-tshshsh!" before the lesson actually began. One day, Plyapa told us about irrational numbers, and I remember weeping, banging my fists on the table and howling, "I don't want $\sqrt{-1}$! Get me out of $\sqrt{-1}$!" This irrational square root grew into me like something alien, foreign and terrifying. It was eating me up and it couldn't be interpreted or rendered harmless, because it was beyond *ratio*.

And now $\sqrt{-1}$ had come back again. I revised my notes, and I realised that I had been too clever; I had been lying to myself just so as not to see $\sqrt{-1}$. It had been all rubbish about being ill and so forth: I could easily have gone to the Guardians' Bureau. A week ago, I know, I would have gone without a second thought. Why was it that now... Why?

And today too. At exactly 16.10 I was standing in front of a shining glass wall. Above me was the gold, sun-bright, pure glow of letters on the Bureau's sign. Deep inside the glass panels stood a long queue of pale-blue unifas. Their faces were glowing like the icon-lamps in an ancient church: they had come to perform a heroic feat, they had come to sacrifice, on the altar of the Unified State, their loved ones, their friends—themselves. And I? I was eager to join them, to be with them. And I couldn't do it: my legs were deeply welded into the glass flagstones. I stood there, staring stupidly and incapable of moving from my place...

"Hey, mathematician, you're dreaming!"

I started. Two black, laughter-varnished eyes and fat negroid lips were turned my way. R-13 the poet, an old acquaintance, and with him was rosy O.

I turned round angrily (I think that if they had not disturbed me, I would finally have torn that $\sqrt{-1}$ out of myself together with my own flesh and would have gone into the Bureau).

"Not dreaming but if you like, I'm admiring," I said rather harshly.

"All right, all right! You shouldn't be a mathematician, my dear fellow, you should be a poet. Yes, a poet! Really, why don't you transfer to us, to the poets, eh? I can fix you up in no time. Want me to?"

R-13 splutters as he speaks; the words come showering out of his fat lips like spray. Every "p" is a fountain, and his "poets" is a fountain too.

"I've served knowledge in the past and shall continue to do so," I said, scowling. I don't like jokes and I don't understand them, but R-13 has a bad habit of making wisecracks.

"Knowledge indeed! That very knowledge of yours is cowardice. That's all it is. You simply want to build a wall round the infinite, but you're too scared to look over that wall. Yes! As soon as you look out, you shut your eyes. Yes!"

"Walls are the basis of every human..." I began.

R spluttered like a fountain and O gave a round and rosy laugh. I took no notice. Let them laugh—I didn't care. I had no time for that. I needed something with which to harry and stifle that damned $\sqrt{-1}$.

"You know what," I suggested. "Let's go and sit down for a while in my place, and we'll solve some problems". (I remembered yesterday's rest-hour; perhaps it might be like that today.)

O glanced at R, then looked clearly and roundly at me, her cheeks lightly tinged with the delicate, disturbing colour of our tickets.

"But today I... Today I have a ticket for him,"

she said with a nod at R. "And he's busy this evening... So..."

The wet, varnished lips smacked good-naturedly:

"Well, why not? Half an hour'll be enough for us. Isn't that right, O? I've no passion for those problems of yours, so just come to my place and we'll have a chat."

I felt strange being left on my own or, to be more precise, with this new person, a stranger to me, who, only by a strange freak of chance, happened to have my number, D-503. I went to his place. True, he was vague, he wasn't rhythmic, he had a kind of amusing, inside-out logic, but nevertheless we were friends. It was no accident that three years ago he and I together had chosen that nice, rosy O. This bound us even more firmly together than our school years.

Later on, in R's room. Everything seemed exactly as it was in my own: a Tablet, the glass of armchairs, table, cupboard and bed. But as soon as he came in, he moved one chair, then another; the planes were displaced, everything left its established confines and became non-Euclidean. R was the same as ever, exactly the same. He had always been at the tail-end in Taylor and mathematics.

We recalled old Plyapa: how we, as little boys, would paste his glass legs all over with thank-you notes (we were very fond of Plyapa). We remembered the Law Teacher. Ours had been exceptionally loud-voiced; it was like a wind came blowing out of the loudspeaker, and we children used to shout the texts after him at the top of our voices. We recalled how our daredevil R had stuffed some chewed paper into the horn, and so a projectile shot out with every word of the text. R was, of course, punished: it had been a vile trick, needless to say. But now we roared with laughter, the whole of our triangle and, I must admit, myself included.

"What if he'd been human, the same as the ancients used to have, eh? Then there'd have been..." A fountain from the fat, smacking lips with every "b"...

Sunshine through the ceiling and the walls; sunshine from above, from the sides, and reflected from below. O sitting on R-13's knees and tiny droplets of sunshine in her blue eyes. I warmed up a little and recovered my balance. $\sqrt{-1}$ had gone mute and was showing no signs of life.

"So how's your *Integral*? Are we going to fly off soon to educate other planet-dwellers, eh? Get a move on, get a move on! Or we poets'll churn out more than your *Integral* can lift. Every day from eight to eleven..." R jerked his head up and scratched the back of it, which was a kind of four-cornered suitcase attached from behind (I was reminded of an ancient picture, "In the Carriage").

I brightened up.

"Ah, so you're writing for *Integral* too, are you? Tell me, what about? Today, for instance."

"Today, nothing. I've been busy with something else..." The "b" spluttered straight at me.

"What with?"

R scowled.

"What with, what with! All right, if you must, with a court sentence. I've been making poetry of a sentence. One idiot, one of our poets... He lived next to me for two years and everything seemed all right. Then, suddenly, this is what he chucks at me: 'I,' says he, 'am a genius, a genius, and I'm above the law.' The things he was saying!.. Oh, what the hell... Ugh!"

The fat lips were dangling, the varnish in the eyes had been eaten away. R-13 jumped up, turned round and stared through the wall at something. I watched his tightly locked suitcase and thought, "What's he sorting over in it now?"

A minute of awkward, asymmetrical silence. I was uncertain what it was all about, but there was something in it.

"Fortunately, the antediluvian times of all possible kinds of Shakespeare and Dostoyevsky, or whatever their names were, have passed," I said in a deliberately loud voice.

R looked round at me. The words sprayed and spurted from him as before, but it seemed to me that the merry varnish had gone from his eyes.

"Yes, my dear mathematician, fortunately, fortunately, fortunately! We are the happiest arithmetical mean... As you people say, integrated from zero to infinity, from the cretin to Shakespeare... Just so!"

I don't know why—it seems totally irrelevant—but I remembered her, the tone of her voice, a very fine thread running between her and R. (Thread of what?) $\sqrt{-1}$ began coming to life again. I opened my plaque: 16 hours 25 minutes. 45 minutes to go before their rose ticket expired.

49

"Well, it's time I went..." I kissed O, shook R's hand and went to the lift.

Even as I was crossing over to the other side of the prospekt, I looked round. In the bright, sun-drenched glass bulk of the house, there were the grey-blue, opaque rectangles of lowered blinds here and there, the rectangles of rhythmic Taylorised happiness. I looked for R-13's window on the seventh floor: he had already lowered his blinds.

Dear O... Dear R... There's something about him also (don't know why "also", but let it be written as it is written), there's something about him also that isn't quite clear to me. Nevertheless, O, he and I form a triangle, even if one with unequal sides, but a triangle nevertheless. To use the language of our ancestors (perhaps you, my readers on other planets, will find this language more understandable), we are a family. And it is so nice sometimes simply to relax for a little while, to lock oneself up in a simple, firm triangle away from everything that...

Entry No. 9
Summary:

LITURGY. IAMBS AND A TROCHEE. THE CAST-IRON HAND.

A solemn, bright day. On such a day you forget your weakness, inaccuracies and ills; everything is crystal-clear, unshakeable and permanent, like our new glass.

Cube Place. The sixty-six mighty concentric circles of the tribunes. And sixty-six rows: the soft lamps of faces, eyes reflecting the glow of the heavens, or, perhaps the glow of the Unified State. Flowers as red as blood: the lips of women. The tender garlands of children's faces in the front rows, close to the scene of the action. A deepened, grim, concentrated Gothic silence.

To judge by the descriptions that have come down to us, something of the kind was experienced by the ancients during their "religious services". But they were worshipping their senseless, unknown God, whereas we serve what is sensible and known in the subtlest sense. Their God gave them nothing but eternal, anguished searchings; their God could think of nothing more clever than that for some inexplicable reason—He should sacrifice Himself. Whereas we sacrifice ourselves to our God, the Unified State, and our sacrifice is calm, considered and rational. Yes, this was a solemn religious service to the Unified State, a remembrance of the agony of the Two Hundred Years War, a majestic celebration of the victory of all over one, of the sum total over the unit...

A man was standing on the steps of the sun-drenched Cube. A white—no, not even white—a colourless face of glass with glass lips. And only the eyes—black, sucking in, gulping down holes and that eerie world from which he was only a few minutes away. His gold plaque had already been removed and his arms bound with a purple ribbon (an ancient custom: the explanation was,

51

apparently, that in antiquity, when all this was being done, but not in the name of the Unified State, the condemned understandably felt themselves entitled to resist and their hands were usually bound with manacles).

Above, on the Cube, near the Machine, sits the motionless, as if cast in metal, figure of him whom we call the Benefactor. From here, down below, the face is indistinguishable: all that can be seen is its stern, majestic square outlines. But the hands... It is sometimes like that in photographs: the hands are too near, they are in the foreground, so that they appear enormous, rivetting the gaze and blotting out everything else. Those heavy hands, calmly resting for the time being on the knees, are clearly of stone, and the knees can barely sustain the weight of them...

Suddenly, one of those enormous hands slowly rose in a slow, cast-iron gesture and, in obedience to the uplifted hand, a number walked up to the Cube. This was one of the State Poets whose happy lot it is to crown the festival with his verse. The divine brass iambics boomed out over the tribunes, telling about the crazed one with the glass eyes who was standing there on the steps and waiting for the logical consequence of his megalomania.

...A conflagration. In the iambics, houses rock, hurl liquid gold to the skies and crash down. Green trees writhe, the sap drips, nothing remains except for the black crosses of burial vaults. But

Prometheus has appeared (it is, of course, our-selves):

And harnessed fire to machine, to steel,
And fettered chaos with the law.

Everything is new, of steel: a steel sun, steel trees, steel people. Suddenly, some madman has "unchained the fire and set it free", and every-thing shall perish again...

Unfortunately, I have a bad memory for verse, but I can definitely remember one thing: it would not have been possible to choose more instructive and beautiful images.

Again a slow, weighty gesture, and a second poet appeared on the steps. I even half-rose in my seat. Impossible! But no, those were his fat, ne-groid lips. It was he... Why hadn't he mentioned before that he was to perform a lofty... His lips were grey and quivering. I could understand why. Before the Benefactor in person, before the entire host of the Guardians... Even so, to be so agi-tated...

Curt, rapid trochaics like the chopping of an axe. About an unprecedented crime: about blas-phemous verses in which the Benefactor had been named... No, I cannot bring my hand to copy them out.

Pale, without looking at anyone (I would never have expected such modesty of him), R-13 de-scended the steps and sat down. For one tiny dif-ferential of a second, I had a glimpse of some-one's face beside him—a sharp black triangle— but it was erased immediately afterwards: my eyes, and thousands of others, were straining upwards, towards the Machine. Up there, the inhuman hand made a third iron gesture. And, wavering in an invisible wind, the criminal walked slowly up: one step, then another, and finally the pace that was to be the last one in his life; and there he was, his face turned to the sky, his head thrown back on his last resting-place.

The Benefactor, as ponderous and rock-like as fate, walked round the Machine and laid an enormous hand on the lever... Not a rustle, not a breath: all eyes were on that hand. What a fiery, clutching whirlwind it must be—to be a tool, to be the resultant of hundreds of thousands of volts. What a great destiny!

An immeasurable second. The hand sank down as it switched on the current. The intolerably sharp beam of a blade flashed like a tremor, a scarcely audible crack in the pipes of the Machine. A spread-eagled body, all in a light, glowing mist, and now it was melting before our eyes, melting, dissolving with appalling rapidity. And then—nothing: just a puddle of chemically pure water that, only a moment ago, had been throbbing tempestuously and redly in a human heart...

All this was simple, all this was known to every one of us: yes, the dissociation of matter, yes, the splitting of the atoms of the human body. Yet every time it was like a miracle, it was like a sign of the Benefactor's inhuman power.

Up above, before Him, were the flushed faces of ten female numbers, lips half-open in excitement, flowers swaying in the breeze[1].

In accordance with the old custom, ten women were adorning with flowers the Benefactor's still bespattered unifa. With the majestic gait of a high priest, slowly He descended the staircase, slowly He walked between the stands, and behind Him followed the upraised, tender white branches of women's arms and the storm of a million shouts sounding as one. And then similar shouts in honour of the host of Guardians, invisibly present here and there in our ranks. Who knows: perhaps it was they, the Guardians, who had been envisioned by the fantasy of ancient man, creating its own gentle yet terrible "archangels", one of whom was appointed to each human being at birth.

Yes, there was something from the ancient religions in this ceremony, something cleansing, like a thunderstorm and a gale. You who happen to be reading this, are you familiar with such moments? I pity you if you don't know them...

[1] From the Botanic Museum, of course. I personally see nothing beautiful in flowers or in anything else that belongs to the savage world, long banished behind the Green Wall. Only the reasonable and useful is beautiful: machines, boots, formulae, food and so forth.

Summary:

LETTER. MEMBRANE.
THE SHAGGY SELF.

Yesterday was for me the kind of paper through which chemists filter their solutions: all the suspended particles, everything superfluous is left behind on it. In the morning, I came down feeling distilled and transparent.

Below, at her desk in the vestibule, the woman on duty was glancing at her watch and writing down the numbers of those coming in. Her name was U... But then I'd better not give her own number, because I'm afraid I might write something bad about her. Although, in fact, she is a very respectable elderly woman. The only thing I don't like about her is that her cheeks sag somewhat, like a fish's gills (is that really so bad?).

She scratched away with her pen and I saw myself on the page: "D-503", with a blot nearby. I was just about to draw her attention to this when she suddenly raised her head and dropped me a kind of an inky smile.

"Here's a letter for you. Take it, my dear, yes, yes, take it."

I knew that the letter she had read still had to go through the Guardians' Bureau (I think it would be superfluous to explain this natural procedure) and would be with me not later than 12. But I was embarrassed by that very smile; the ink-blot had clouded my clear solution. So much so that later, at the *Integral* shipyard, I could not concentrate at all and once even made a mistake in my calculations, something which had never happened to me before.

At 12 o'clock, again the pinkish-brown fish-gills, the little smile, and I had the letter in my hands at last. I don't know why I didn't read it on the spot but pushed it into my pocket instead and hurried up to my room. I opened it, glanced through it and—sat down... It was an official notification to the effect that Number I-330 had been assigned to me and that I must report to her at 21, at the address stated below...

No, after all that had happened, after I had so unequivocally shown my attitude to her. Moreover, she didn't even know whether I had been to the Guardians' Bureau; after all, she had no way of knowing that I had been ill, and in general I just couldn't... And yet, in spite of everything...

A dynamo was spinning and humming in my head. The Buddha—yellow lilies-of-the-valley—a rosy crescent... Yes, and another thing: O wanted to call on me today. Was I to show her this notification about I-330? I didn't know. She wouldn't believe (how, indeed, could she?) that I didn't have anything to do with this, that I was completely... I knew: there would be a difficult, foolish, utterly illogical conversation... No, anything but that. Let it all be decided routinely: I would simply send her a copy of the notification.

I hurriedly thrust the notification into my

pocket and saw that horrible, ape's hand of mine. I remembered how she, I-330, had taken hold of my hand during the promenade and had looked at it. Did she really...

It was now a quarter to 21. A white night. Everything was like green glass. But this was a different, fragile glass, not ours, not real. It was a thin glass shell, and under it life was spinning, racing, humming... I would not have been surprised if the domes of the auditoriums had risen at that very moment like round, slow puffs of smoke, and the elderly moon had smiled inkily—like the woman at the desk this morning—and all the blinds in all the houses had been lowered simultaneously, and behind the blinds—

A strange sensation. I could feel my ribs—they were like iron wands and they were hampering, positively hampering my heart: too tight, not enough room. I was standing before a glass door marked "I-330" in gold lettering. She had her back to me and was bending over the desk to write something. I went in...

"Here..." I proffered the rose ticket. "I received a notification this morning, and I have reported."

"How punctual you are! In a moment, is that all right? Take a seat, I'll just finish this."

She looked down at the letter again. What was there within her, behind the lowered blinds? What was she going to say, what was she going to do in a moment? How was I to learn this and compute it when all of her was from beyond, from the wild and ancient land of dreams?

I looked at her in silence. My ribs were iron wands, too tight... When she spoke, her face was like a fast, flashing wheel: you can't see the separate spokes. But now the wheel was at rest. And I could see a strange combination: the dark brows raised high at the temples—a mocking, sharp triangle with its apex pointing upwards, and two deep, thin lines from the nose to the corners of the mouth. And those two triangles seemed to contradict one another; they marked her whole face with an unpleasant, irritating x, like a cross: a face that had been crossed out.

The wheel began turning, the spokes blurred...

"So you didn't go to the Guardians' Bureau?"

"I was... I couldn't. I was ill."

"Yes, I thought so. Something was bound to prevent you, no matter what (sharp teeth, a smile). Anyway you're in my hands now. Remember: 'Any number that does not report to the Bureau within 48 hours is considered...'"

My heart beat so hard that the wands bent. Like a little boy, as foolishly as a little boy, I had fallen for it, I was foolishly silent. I felt entangled, and it was no use trying to struggle...

She stood up and stretched lazily. She pressed a button and the blinds fell on all sides with a faint crack. I was cut off from the world: she and I were alone together.

She was somewhere behind me, near the wardrobe. A unifa rustled and fell. I was listening. And I remembered... No, it flashed across my mind in a hundredth of a second...

I had recently had occasion to calculate the curve for a street membrane of a new type (these membranes, elegantly decorated, are now on all the prospekts, recording street conversations for the Guardians' Bureau). And I remembered a concave, pink, quivering eardrum, a strange creature, consisting of only one organ—the ear. I was now such a membrane myself.

A button popped at the collar, another on her breast, another still lower. The glassy silk rustled over her shoulders, over her knees, over the floor. I heard, more clearly than if I was seeing, one foot and then the other stepping out of the blue-grey pile of silk...

The tautly stretched membrane was trembling and recording the silence. No: abrupt, with infinite pauses, blows of a hammer on the wands. And I could hear—I could see: she was thinking, for a moment, behind me.

Sound of the wardrobe door, a lid banged, and again silk, silk...

"Now then, please."

I looked round. She was wearing a light saf-fron-yellow dress of an ancient pattern. It was a thousand times more evil than if she had been wearing nothing at all. Two sharp points through the flimsy fabric, glowing rosily-two coals through the cinders. Two softly rounded knees...

She was sitting in a low armchair. On the four-cornered table in front of her stood a flagon containing something poisonously green and two tiny glasses on stems. Smoking in the corner of her mouth was a thin paper tube, that ancient smoking (I forgot what it's called).

The membrane was still quivering. The hammer was thudding in there, inside me, against the red-hot wands. I could hear each blow distinctly and ... had she suddenly heard it herself?

But she calmly went on smoking, calmly glancing at me from time to time. Then she casually flicked the ash—on to my pink ticket.

I asked as composedly as possible:

"Listen, in this case, why did you put your name down for me? And why did you make me come here?"

It was as if she hadn't even heard. She filled one of the tiny glasses and sipped.

"A delightful liqueur. Would you care for some?"

Only at this point did I realise that it was alcohol. Yesterday's picture flashed in front of my eyes: the stone hand of the Benefactor, the intolerable blade of the light-ray, but there, on the Cube, that spreadeagled body with the head thrown back. I shuddered.

"Listen," I said. "You know perfectly well that all who poison themselves with nicotine, and especially with alcohol—the Unified State is merciless..."

The dark brows shot up towards the temples, the sharp triangle of a smile:

"To annihilate a few quickly is more rational than to give many the opportunity for self-destruction, degeneration and so on. It's true to the point of indecency."

"Yes ... to the point of indecency."

"But this bevy of bald-headed, naked truths—to let them out on to the street... No, just imagine... Just take my admirer—yes, you know him—and imagine him casting off all the falsity of clothing and showing himself in his true form in public... Ugh!"

She was laughing... But I could clearly see her funereal lower triangle: two deep folds from the corners of the mouth to the nose. And, for some reason, those folds made it clear to me that the double-bent, round-shouldered and bat-eared one used to embrace her just as she was now... He...

Incidentally, I am trying to convey my abnormal sensations as they were at the time. Now, as I write this, I am perfectly well aware that all this should have been so and that he, like any honourable number, was entitled to his joys—and it would be unjust... Anyway, that's clear.

She laughed very strangely and for a long time. Then she looked intently at and into me.

"What matters most is that I am completely at my ease with you. You're so nice. Oh, I'm sure of one thing: you won't even dream of going to the Bureau and reporting that I drink liqueur and smoke. You'll be unwell, or you'll be busy, or I don't know what. And, what's more, I'm convinced you will now drink this charming poison with me..."

What a brazen, derisive tone of voice. I definitely felt that I now hated her again. But why "now"? I had hated her all the time.

She tilted the whole glass of green poison into her mouth, stood up and, shining pink through the saffron, took a few steps and stopped behind my armchair...

Suddenly, an arm round my neck and her lips on mine... No, somewhere even deeper, even more terrifying... I swear I was not expecting anything like this, and, perhaps, only because... After all, I couldn't have—I now understand this quite clearly—I couldn't have wanted what happened next.

Intolerably sweet lips (the taste of the "liqueur", presumably) and a mouthful of burning poison was poured into me—then more, and more and more... I unstrapped myself from the ground and, revolving frenziedly like an independent planet, was borne down and down in an uncalculated orbit...

What happened next I can only describe approximately, by means of more or less close analogies.

Somehow this had never entered my head before, but after all, that's the way it is: we on Earth are walking all the time over a gurgling, purple sea of fire hidden down below in the depths of the planet. We never even think about it. But suddenly it's as if the thin shell underfoot had turned into glass and suddenly we can see...

I became glass. I saw into myself from outside.

There were two of me. One was the former I, Number D-503, whereas the other... Formerly, he had only poked his hairy paws a little way out of the shell, but now the whole of him was crawling out, the shell was cracking, it would fly to pieces at any moment and... And then what?

Clutching with all my might at a straw—the arms of the chair—I asked, so as to hear myself, my former self:

"Where... Where did you get this ... this poison?"

"Oh, this! Just a medic, one of my..."

"'One of my'"? 'One of my' what?"

Then the other me suddenly jumped out and roared:

"I won't allow it! I don't want anyone but me. I'll kill every man who... Because it's you, you that I..."

I saw him roughly seize her with his hairy paws, rip apart the thin silk on her and sink his teeth in—I remember it distinctly: his teeth.

I don't know how she managed it, but she wriggled free. And now her eyes were covered by that confounded blind. She stood there, leaning back against the wardrobe and listening to me.

I remember being on the floor, embracing her legs, kissing her knees. And praying, "Now, now, this minute..."

Sharp teeth, and the sharp, mocking triangle of the brows. She bent down and silently unfastened my plaque.

"Yes! Yes, my darling, my darling!" I began hastily throwing off my unifa. But, just as silently, she raised the watch on my plaque till it was level with my eyes. it was five minutes short of 22.30.

My blood went cold. I knew what this meant:

64

appearing on the streets after 22.30. All my madness suddenly seemed to be blown away. I was myself again. One thing was clear to me: I hated her, I hated her, I hated her!

Without saying goodbye, without looking back, I rushed straight out of the room. Somehow pinning my plaque on again as I ran, going down the back stairs two at a time (I was afraid I might meet someone in the lift), I rushed out on to the empty prospekt.

Everything was as simple, ordinary and legitimate as usual: the glass houses, brilliant with lights, the pale glass sky and the green, motionless night. But something turbulent, purple and hairy was rushing soundlessly along under that quiet, cool glass. And I, panting for breath, raced on so as not to be late.

Suddenly, I felt my hastily pinned-on plaque coming loose: it detached itself and rang on the glass pavement. I bent down to pick it up, and in the momentary silence, I heard someone's footsteps behind me. I looked round. Something small and bent was coming round a corner. Or so it seemed to me at the time.

I ran as fast as I could, conscious of nothing but a whistling in my ears. I stopped at the entrance. It was one minute to 22.30 by my watch. I listened, but there was no one behind. It had all been a silly fantasy, the effect of the poison.

That night was torture. The bed under me kept rising, then falling, then rising again, as if floating on a sine wave. I kept telling myself: "At night,

65

the numbers must sleep: it is an obligation, like work in the daytime. It is essential so that work can be done in the daytime. Not to sleep at night is a crime..." But I still couldn't sleep, I just couldn't.

I'm done for. I'm unable to fulfil my obligations to the Unified State... I...

Entry No. 11
Summary:
...NO, I CAN'T, LET IT BE WITHOUT A SUMMARY.

Evening. A light mist. The sky is draped with a milky-golden fabric and it isn't possible to see what is beyond, higher up. The ancients knew that the greatest and most bored sceptic of all was up there—God. We know that beyond is a crystal-blue, stark, unseemly nothing. I do not know what is beyond there, for I learned too much. Knowledge, absolutely certain of its infallibility, is faith. I had firm faith in myself, I believed that I knew everything in myself. And now...

I am in front of the mirror. And for the first time in my life, for the very first time, I can see myself clearly, distinctly, consciously: I see myself with amazement as one who is somebody else. There I am—him: black brows drawn in a straight line; between them, like a scar, a vertical furrow (I don't know whether it was there before). Steely grey eyes encircled with the shadows of a sleepless night; and behind that steel ... apparently, I never knew what was there. And from "there" (this "there" is simultaneously here and infinitely far away), from "there" I look at myself—at him, and I know full well that he, the one with the brows drawn in a straight line, is an outsider, is a stranger to me, I have met him for the first time in my life. But I am real, I am not him...

No: full stop. This is all nonsense, and all these stupid sensations are a fever, the result of being poisoned yesterday... By what? By a swallow of green fluid, or by her? It's all the same. I am noting this down only to show how strangely the human reason, so precise and keen, can become confused and lose its way. The reason which could make even this infinity, so frightening to the ancients, into something digestible, by means of...

A click of the numerator and the characters R-13. So be it, I'm even glad. On my own just now I would be feeling...

20 minutes later:

On the flat of paper, in the two-dimensional world—these lines are close to me, but in another world... I am losing my sense of numbers: 20 minutes might be 200 or 200,000. And it's so weird: calmly, deliberately thinking over every word and writing down what happened between me and R. It's exactly the same as if you were sitting with your legs crossed in an armchair by your own bed and were watching with curiosity the way that you—yes, you—are writhing on that bed.

When R-13 came in, I was completely calm and normal. With a feeling of sincere rapture, I began talking about how magnificently he had managed to put the sentence into trochaics and it was more by those trochaics of his that the madman had been cut to pieces and eliminated.

"...And even this: if it was proposed that I should make a schematic drawing of the Benefactor's Machine, I would surely, but surely, somehow manage to put your trochaics on that drawing," I concluded.

Suddenly I saw R's eyes going dull and his lips turning grey.

"What's the matter with you?"

"What? Why... Why, I'm simply fed up: nothing around but death sentences. I don't want to hear any more, that's all there is to it. I don't want to!"

He frowned and rubbed the back of his head, that little suitcase full of extraneous luggage that I didn't understand. A pause. At last he found something in the suitcase, pulled it out, untied it and unfolded it; his eyes became varnished with laughter and he jumped to his feet.

"And here am I, composing for your *Integral* ... this— Yes, this is really something!"

He was his old self: his lips smacking and spraying, the words spluttering like a fountain.

"Please understand (the "p" was a fountain), the ancient legend of paradise... You see, it's about us, about the now. Yes! Think hard about it. Those two in paradise were given a choice: happiness without freedom, or freedom without happiness.. There was no third choice. And they, the numskulls, chose freedom, and so, understandably, they yearned over the ages for fetters. For fetters, that's what the world's grief is about. Over the ages! And only we guessed how to bring back happiness... No, listen further, let me carry on! The ancient God and we are sitting together at the same table. Yes! We have helped God to overcome the devil once and for all—after all, it was he who prompted people to break the ban and taste fatal freedom, he, the evil serpent. But we stamp on his head—crunch! And it's done; paradise again. And again we're naive and innocent, like Adam and Eve. None of that muddle about good and evil: everything is very simple, paradisaically, childishly simple. The Benefactor, the Machine, the Cube, the Gas Belli the Guardians—all this is good, all this is magnificent, beautiful, noble, exalted, crystal-pure. Because this protects our non-freedom, that is, our happiness. The ancients at this point would begin to criticise, to reason, to cudgel their brains: ethical, unethical... Well, all right; in a word, here's a heavenly little poem for you, eh? And yet the tone is most serious... You understand? It really is something, is it not?"

As if I couldn't understand! I remember thinking, "He's so absurd and asymmetrical to look at, and he has such a correctly thinking mind. That's why he's so close to me, to the real me (I still regard my former self as the real one; everything of the present is, of course, merely a disease).

R evidently read this on my brow, embraced me by the shoulders and burst out laughing.

"Oh, you... Adam! Yes, by the way, about Eve..."

He rummaged in his pocket, drew out a notebook and leafed through it.

"The day after tomorrow... No, in two days' time, O has a rose ticket to visit you. So how d'you feel about it? The same as before? D'you want her to..."

"Yes, obviously."

"I'll tell her. She's too shy herself, you see... What a story, I must say! She only visits me on a rose ticket basis, but as for you... And she doesn't say that this is a fourth person that's crept into our triangle. Who—repent, you sinner, well?"

A curtain shot up inside me and—the rustle of silk, the green flask, the lips... And quite irrelevantly, for no reason at all, I burst out with (if only I had held my tongue!):

"Tell me, have you ever tried nicotine or alcohol?"

R pursed his lips and looked at me from under his brows. I could distinctly hear his thoughts: "You're a friend, of course... But even so..." And the answer:

"How am I to put it? Frankly, no. But I knew a woman..."

"I-330!" I exclaimed.

"What? You ... you've been with her as well?"

he dissolved into laughter, choked and was about to spray me at any moment.

My mirror was hanging in such a way that you could only look into it across the table: from my place in the armchair, I could only see my forehead and eyebrows.

And I, the real one, saw a distorted, jumping straight line of eyebrows in the mirror, and the real I heard a savage, disgusting shriek:

"What d'you mean, 'as well'? No, what's this 'as well'? No, I demand to know."

Stretched negroid lips. Bulging eyes... The real I clutched the collar of that other self, the savage, hairy, panting I. The real I said to R:

"Forgive me, for the Benefactor's sake. I'm not at all well, I can't get any sleep. I don't know what's the matter with me..."

The fat lips grinned fleetingly:

"Yes, yes, yes! I understand, I understand! I'm familiar with all this ... in theory, of course. Goodbye!"

In the doorway, he spun round like a black ball, then rushed back to the table and threw a book on to it.

"My latest... Brought it specially, nearly forgot. Goodbye..." The "b" sprayed me with spittle and he rolled out of the room.

I was alone. Or, to be more precise, I was alone with that other "I". I was in an armchair and, crossing my legs, I looked with curiosity from a kind of "over there" at myself, yes, at myself writhing on the bed.

71

Why, but why had O and I for three whole years been living on such friendly terms, and then, suddenly, only one word about that other woman, about... Was all this madness of love and jealousy not just something in those ridiculous ancient books? And most important of all, I! Equations, formulae, figures and ... now this. I couldn't understand a thing! Not a thing ... Tomorrow I would go to R and tell him that...

No, it wasn't true, I wouldn't go. I wouldn't call on him any more, neither tomorrow nor the day after. I couldn't and didn't want to see him. It was the end! Our triangle had fallen apart.

I was alone. Evening. A slight mist. The sky draped with a milky gold fabric. If only I knew what was up there beyond. If only I knew who I was and what I was like.

Entry No. 12
Summary:

LIMITATION OF INFINITY.
THE ANGEL. REFLECTIONS
ON POETRY.

It still seems to me that I will recuperate, that I can recuperate. I slept beautifully. None of those dreams or other morbid phenomena. My dear O will visit me tomorrow, everything will be as simple, correct and finite as a circle. I'm not afraid of that word "finiteness": the work of the highest thing in man, the reason, boils precisely down to the uninterrupted limitation of infinity, to the fragmentation of infinity into convenient, easily digestible portions, or differentials. This is the divine beauty of my element—mathematics. And an understanding of this beauty is precisely what I-330 does not have. Incidentally, this is just a chance association.

All this to the measured, metric rumble of the wheels on the underground. I mentally chanted the rhythm of the wheels, and also verse (that book of his yesterday). And I sensed that behind me, over my shoulder, someone was cautiously bending down and looking at the open pages. Without looking round, solely out of the corner of my eye, I saw pink, outspread ear-wings, the double-curved... It was him! I didn't want to disturb him, so I pretended not to notice. I don't know how he turned up here: he had not been there when I had entered the carriage.

This essentially insignificant occurrence had a particularly good effect on me; I would say it even fortified me. It is so pleasant to be aware of someone's keen gaze, lovingly protecting one from the slightest mistake, from the slightest false step. This may sound somewhat sentimental, but the same analogy comes into my head again: the guardian angels about whom the ancients dreamed. So much of what they only dreamed has become reality in our own life.

At the moment when I sensed the guardian angel behind me, I was enjoying a sonnet entitled "Happiness". I don't think I shall be mistaken if

I say that it is of rare beauty and depth. Here are the first four lines:

Ever enamoured two times two,
Ever fused in a passionate four,
And the world's most passionate pair
Make an inseparable two times two...

All the rest is about this: the wise, eternal happiness of the multiplication table.

Every genuine poet is invariably a Columbus. Even before Columbus, America had existed for ages, but only Columbus managed to find it. The multiplication table had existed for centuries before R-13 too, but only R-13 was able to find the new Eldorado in a virgin forest of figures. Indeed, is happiness anywhere more wise, more cloudless than in this miraculous world? Steel rusts; the ancient God created ancient—i.e. prone to err—man and, as a consequence, Himself committed an error. The multiplication table is wiser, more absolute than the ancient God: it never, you understand, but never makes a mistake. And no figures are happier than the ones that live according to the harmonious eternal laws of the multiplication table. No vacillations, no errors. The truth is one and the way is one; and this truth is two times two, and this true way is four. And would it not be an absurdity if these happily, ideally multiplied two's began thinking about some kind of freedom, that is, only too clearly about a mistake? For me it is axiomatic that R-13 was able to grasp what was most fundamental, what was most...

Here I again felt, first on the back of my head

then on my left ear, the warm, gentle breath of the guardian angel. He had clearly noticed that the book on my knees was already closed and my thoughts were far away. Why, I was ready to open the pages of my brain before him at any moment; it was such a calm, consolatory feeling. I remember I even looked round, I stared insistently and hopefully into his eyes, but he didn't understand, or didn't want to understand, and he didn't ask me any questions... I only have one thing left: to tell all to you, my unknown reader (at this moment you are as dear and close and inaccessible as he was at that moment).

That was my path: from the part to the whole; the part was R-13, the majestic whole was our Institute of State Poets and Writers. I thought of how it could happen that the ancients were never struck by the fatuousness of their literature and poetry. The enormous, magnificent power of the creative word was wasted on absolutely nothing. It was simply ridiculous: each wrote about whatever occurred to him. Just as ridiculously and fatuously as the fact that the sea which, in the time of the ancients, beat fatuously on the coast all round the clock and the billions of kilogrammometres locked up in the waves went merely on warming the feelings of lovers. From the enamoured whisper of the waves we obtained electricity, from the wild beast frenziedly foaming at the mouth we bred the domestic animal: and exactly in the same way we have tamed and saddled the once wild element of poetry. Poetry is no longer a brazen whistling of the nightingale: poetry is state service, poetry is utility.

Our famous "Mathematical Nones"—could we have so sincerely and tenderly loved the four rules of arithmetic in school without them? And "Thorns" is a classical image: the Guardians are the thorns on the rose, protecting the delicate Flower of the State from rude contact... What heart of stone will remain indifferent to innocent childish lips murmuring like a prayer: "The nasty boy, he grabs a rose. The steel thorn pricks, the red blood flows. Ow, ow! And home full pelt he goes," and so on? And the "Daily Odes to the Benefactor"? Who, on reading them, will not bow his head piously before the self-sacrificing toil of that Number of Numbers? And the eerie red "Blossoms of the Court Sentences"? And the immortal tragedy, "He Was Late For Work"? And that coffee-table book, "Stanzas on Sexual Hygiene"?

The whole of life in all its complexity and beauty has been hammered out forever in the gold of words.

Our poets no longer coast about in the empyrean: they have come down to Earth; they keep in step with us to the strict mechanical march of the Music Factory; their lyre is the morning chatter of electric toothbrushes, the ominous crackle of sparks in the Benefactor's Machine, and the magnificent echo of the Anthem of the Unified State, and the intimate ring of the shining crystalline chamber pot, and the exciting rattle of falling blinds, and the cheerful voices of the latest cookery book, and the almost inaudible whisper of the street membranes.

Our gods are here, with us, in the Bureau, in the kitchen, in the workshop, in the toilet. The gods have become like us: *ergo*, we have become like the gods. And to you, my unknown planetary readers, we are coming to make your life as divinely rational and precise as our own...

Entry No. 13
Summary:
MIST. A COMPLETELY STUPID OCCURRENCE.

I woke at dawn, and a rosy, tough firmament met my eyes. Everything was good and round. O would come in the evening. I was undoubtedly fit already. I smiled and fell asleep again.

The morning bell. I got up, and everything was different: through the glass of the ceiling and the walls I could see that everything was permeated with mist. The crazy clouds were getting heavier and heavier, and lighter, and nearer until there was no division between earth and sky; everything was flying, melting, falling, there was nothing to get hold of. No more houses: the glass walls had dissolved in the mist, like salt crystals in water. If you looked up from the pavement, the dark shapes of people in the houses, like weighed particles in a feverish milky solution, hung lower, and higher, and still higher, on the tenth storey. And everything was smoking—perhaps it was a soundlessly raging fire.

11.45 precisely: I deliberately glanced at my watch to clutch at the figures so that they would rescue me.

At 11.45, before proceeding, as required by the Tablet of the Hours, to physical exercises, I ran into the room. Suddenly, the phone ringing and a woman's voice—a long, slow needle in the heart.

"Aha, you're at home? I'm very glad. Wait for me on the corner. We'll leave together for... Well, you'll see in due course."

"You know perfectly well I'm going to work."

"You know perfectly well you'll do just as I tell you. I'll be seeing you. In two minutes..."

Two minutes later, I was standing on the corner. But she had to be shown that I was controlled by the Unified State, not by her. "Just as I tell you..." And she is absolutely sure: I can tell it from her voice. Well, I'll give her a proper talking to...

Grey unifas, woven of damp mist, hurriedly materialised beside me for a moment and suddenly dissolved into the mist. I never took my eyes off my watch, I was a sharp, trembling second-hand. Eight, ten minutes... Three minutes to twelve, two minutes to twelve...

Of course, I was already late for work. How I hated her. But I really had to show her...

On the corner in the white mist—blood, a cross-section cut with a sharp knife—lips.

"I've kept you waiting, apparently. Anyway, it doesn't matter. You're already too late."

How I hated her-but it was already too late.

I looked in silence at her lips. All women are lips, just lips. Some have rosy ones, sinuously round: a ring, a gentle barrier from the whole world. And these: a moment ago they didn't even exist, and only just this moment—like a knife-slash, and the sweet blood was still dripping.

She came nearer and leaned her shoulder against mine, and we were one, there was a transfusion from her into me, and I knew it had to be. I knew with each nerve, each hair, each painfully sweet beat of the heart. And it was such joy to submit to that "had to be". A piece of iron is probably just as joyful at submitting to the inevitable precise law and fastening on to a magnet. A stone thrown upwards hesitates for a moment and then falls straight down to the ground. And a human being, after the death agony, will sigh for the last time and pass away.

I remember smiling vaguely and saying aimlessly:

"It's misty... Very."

"You like mist?"

"I hate the mist. I fear the mist."

"That means you love it. You fear it because it's stronger than you, you hate it because you fear it, you love it because you cannot dominate it. You see, it's only possible to love the indomitable."

Yes, she's right. Precisely because ... precisely because I...

We were walking along, two of us as one. Somewhere far away through the mist the sun was singing almost inaudibly, everything was being suffused by the resilient, the purple, the gold, the pink and the red. The whole world is a single unencompassable woman, and we are in her very womb, we are not yet born, we are joyfully ripening. And it is clear to me, indestructibly clear, that everything is for me—the sun, the mist, the rosy, the golden—everything is for me...

I didn't ask where we were going. It didn't matter, just so long as we walked and walked, looking, being more and more resiliently suffused...

"Here we are..." She stopped outside a door. "There's a certain man on duty here just now... I mentioned him back there in the Ancient House."

Carefully, with my eyes alone, jealously guarding what was maturing within me, I read the notice, "Medical Bureau". I understood everything.

A glass room full of golden mist. Glass ceilings with coloured bottles and jars. Wires. Bluish sparks in pipes.

And a little man, incredibly thin. He seemed cut entirely out of paper, and whichever way he turned, you only saw the sharply cut-out profile: the flashing blade of the nose, the scissors of the lips.

I couldn't hear what she was saying to him: I was watching the way she talked, and I felt that I was smiling, irrepressibly, blissfully smiling. The blades of the scissor-lips flashed and the doctor said:

"Yes, yes. I understand. A most dangerous disease. I don't know of one more dangerous..." He laughed, wrote something down with a very thin paper hand and gave the sheet to her. Then he wrote something down and handed it to me.

They were to certify that we were ill and could not report for work. I was stealing my work from the Unified State, I was a thief, I was in the shadow of the Benefactor's Machine. And yet it was all remote and of no importance to me, as in a book... I took the sheet of paper without hesitating for a second. I—my eyes, lips and hands—knew this had to be.

We took an aero in a half-empty hangar on the corner, I-330 sat at the wheel again, moved the starter to "forward" and we lifted off from the ground and sailed away. And everything followed us: the rosy-gold mist, the sun, the doctor's finely razor-blade-thin profile, suddenly so beloved and so close. Earlier, everything had been revolving around the sun; but now I knew that everything was revolving around me—slowly, blissfully, with screwed-up eyes...

The old woman at the gates of the Ancient House. That dear, skin-sealed mouth with its wrinkle-rays. It had probably been sealed like that all these days and had only just now opened to smile:

"Ah, naughty-naughty! Not one to work like everybody else... Oh, all right, then! If anything happens, I'll hurry up and tell you..."

The heavy, creaking opaque door closed and at once my heart opened wide with pain and still wider until it was right open. Her lips were mine,

81

I drank and drank, withdrew, looked silently into eyes wide-open to me—and then once more...

The semidarkness of rooms, the dark-blue, saffron yellow, dark-green morocco leather, the golden smile of the Buddha, the flashing of mirrors. And my old dream, so understandable now, all imbued with golden-pink sap that would brim over any moment now and would spill—

It ripened. And as inevitably as iron and magnet, with sweet submissiveness to the exact and immutable law, I flowed into her. There was no rose coupon, there was no account, there was no Unified State, there was no me. There were only tenderly sharp, tight-set teeth, there were golden eyes wide-open and looking at me, and through them I slowly went inside, deeper and deeper. And silence—only in a corner of the room, thousands of miles away, a tap was dripping into the washbasin and I was the universe, and drop was separated from drop by eras, by epochs...

I pulled on my unifa and bent down to her, and I took her into me with my eyes for one last time.

"I knew it... I knew you..." she said, very softly.

She got up quickly, put on her own unifa and her usual sharp vinegar smile.

"Well, fallen angel. You see, you're finished now. You're not afraid, are you? Well, then, till we meet again! You'll go back on your own. All right?"

She opened the mirror-door fitted to the front

of the wardrobe and looked over her shoulder at me, waiting. I obediently went out. But as soon as I had crossed the threshold, I suddenly felt a need for her to press her shoulder against mine—just her shoulder for a moment, nothing more.

I rushed back into the room where she would probably be buttoning up her unifa in front of the mirror. I ran in—and stopped. I could clearly see the ancient wardrobe's key-ring swinging from the lock, but there was no sign of her. She couldn't have gone out: there was only one exit from the room, and yet she was gone. I ran my hands over everything, I even opened the wardrobe and felt the ancient multicoloured dresses in there. Nobody...

I feel embarrassed, my planetary readers, telling you about this perfectly incredible occurrence. But what can I do if that is exactly what happened? After all, hadn't the whole day ever since morning been full of improbabilities? Wasn't it like that ancient disease of dreaming? And if so, what did it matter, one absurdity more or less? Besides, I'm convinced that sooner or later I'll be able to include any absurdity in some kind of syllogism. The thought calms me down, and I hope it will do the same for you.

...How fulfilled I am! If you only knew how fulfilled!

Entry No. 14
Summary:
"MINE". FORBIDDEN.
THE COLD FLOOR.

Still about yesterday. My private hour before sleep was busy and I couldn't write in my diary yesterday. But it's all crystal clear in my mind, and therefore especially—perhaps forever—that intolerably cold floor...

O was supposed to come and see me in the evening; it was her day. I went down to the duty officer to draw the right to lower the blinds.

"What's the matter with you?" asked the duty officer. "You seem a bit off today..."

"I ... I'm ill..."

In fact, it was the truth: I was, of course, ill. The whole thing was an illness. And I promptly remembered: yes, the certificate... I felt in my pocket and it rustled in there. Which meant that it had all happened, it had all really happened.

I handed the paper to the duty officer. I felt my cheeks flame up. Without looking, I could see that he was staring at me in amazement.

Now it was 21.30. The blinds were lowered in the room on the left. In the room on the right, I could see my neighbour bent over a book, his bumpy bald head, and the enormous yellow parabola of his brow. I paced up and down, up and down in torment: how was I going to go about it with O after everything? On the right, I could distinctly feel eyes on me, I could clearly see the furrows on the forehead, a row of yellow, indecipherable lines. And for some reason I imagined those lines were about me.

At a quarter to 22 in my room there was a joyous rosy whirlwind, the firm ring of rosy arms around my neck. But then I felt the ring becoming weaker and weaker; it unlocked itself and the arms sank down.

"You're not the same as you were before, you're not mine!"

"What barbaric terminology—'mine'. I never had been yours..." I stopped short: it occurred to me that I had not been hers earlier, true, but now... Now I was not living in our rational world at all, but in the ancient, delirious world of the square root of minus one.

The blinds fell. Out there, behind the wall on the right, my neighbour dropped his book from the table on to the floor, and through the last, brief narrow chink between blind and floor I saw a yellow hand snatch up the book, and inwardly I wanted to seize hold of that hand with all my strength...

"I was thinking—I wanted to meet you today on the promenade. I have so much to talk about, I have so much to tell you..."

Poor dear O! The rosy mouth, the crescent with its horns turned down. But I couldn't tell her everything that had happened, if only because this would make her a party to my crimes. After all, I know she hasn't the strength to go to the Guardians' Bureau and consequently...

O was lying down. I was kissing her slowly. I kissed that naive, puffy fold on her wrist. The dark-blue eyes were closed, the rosy crescent was slowly opening up and blossoming, and I was kissing her all over.

Suddenly, I clearly felt how devastated and surrendered everything was. I couldn't, it was impossible. I ought to, and it was impossible. My lips promptly went cold...

The rosy crescent trembled, lost lustre, writhed. O pulled the blanket over her, wrapped herself round in it and buried her face in the pillow...

I was sitting beside the bed on the floor—it was such a desperately cold floor, and I was not speaking. An agonising cold from below, coming up higher and higher. Probably the same silent cold as out there in blue, mute, interplanetary space.

"Please try to understand, I didn't mean..." I muttered... "I tried my hardest..."

It was true. The real I hadn't wanted it. Even so, what words could I use to tell her? How was I to explain that the iron didn't want it, but the law was inevitable, precise...

She lifted her face up out of the pillows and, without opening her eyes, she said:

"Go away," but her tears turned the words into "gway", and for some reason even this silly triviality imprinted itself on my mind.

Chilled through and through, numb, I went out into the corridor. The smoke of the mist outside the glass was thin, almost indiscernible. But it would fall again by night, perhaps, and cover everything. What kind of night was it going to be?

O glided silently past me to the lift and the door slammed.

"Just a moment!" I shouted. I was terrified.

But the lift was already rumbling down, down, down...

She had taken R from me.

She had taken O from me.

Yet even so, yet even so.

Entry No. 15
Summary:

THE BELL. THE MIRROR SEA.
I AM TO ROAST ETERNALLY.

No sooner had I walked on to the shipyard where *Integral* was being built than the Second Constructor came to meet me. His face was, as always, round, white, porcelain—a plate, and when he spoke, he held up something intolerably tasty on it.

"You took the liberty of going sick, and without you, without the management yesterday, it may be said that there was an incident here."

"An incident?"

"Yes indeed! The bell rang, they finished work, they began dismissing everybody from the yard, and then just imagine: the supervisor caught a man without a number. I can't understand how he sneaked his way in. He was taken off to the Operating Theatre. They'll screw the why's and wherefore's out of the dear fellow in there." (A tasty smile.)

Our best and most experienced doctors work in the Operating Theatre under the immediate guidance of the Benefactor in person. They've got various instruments in there, especially the famous Gas Bell. It's really an ancient school experiment: a mouse is put under a glass hood and the air is gradually evacuated from the hood by an air-pump... Well, and so on. Except that the Gas Bell is, of course, a more refined apparatus, with the application of various gases and in this case, of course, it's not a trick being played on a defence-less animal, it expresses a lofty ideal—concern for the security of the Unified State. In other words, for the happiness of millions. About five centuries ago, when work in the Operating Theatre was only just being organised, some fools compared the Operating Theatre with the ancient Inquisition, but this really is as incongruous as putting a surgeon performing a tracheotomy on the same level as a highwayman: each may be holding a knife and each may be doing the same thing—cutting the throat of a living human being. But one of them is a benefactor, the other is a criminal: one is marked with a + sign, the other with a - sign...

All this is too clear, all this takes in one second, one revolution of the logic machine; but then the cogs suddenly snag on a minus, and look—something else is already on top: the ring is still swaying on the wardrobe. The door had only just been slammed, and she was gone, she had vanished. This was something a machine could never cope with. A dream? But I could still feel the incomprehensible sweet pain in my right shoulder—she had pressed up against my right shoulder, she was beside me in the mist. "You like mist?" Yes, and the mist too... I love everything, and everything is resilient, new, amazing, everything is good...

"Everything is good," I said aloud.

"Good?" The porcelain eyes bulged roundly. "What's so good about it? If that unnumbered man was clever enough to ... then they ... they're everywhere, around, all the time, they're here, they're close to *Integral*, they..."

"But who are *they?*"

"How should I know? But I can feel them, you understand? All the time."

"Have you heard about the new operation they've invented? They cut out fantasy." (I had indeed heard something of the kind recently.)

"Yes, I know. What's this got to do with it?"

"Why, in your place I'd go and ask them to do this operation on you."

Something as acid as lemon had become plainly discernible on the plate. Dear fellow, he had taken offence at the remote hint that he could have fantasy... But what of it? A week ago, I too would probably have taken offence. Only not now. Because I knew what was wrong with me; I knew that I was ill. And I knew, moreover, that I didn't want to recover. I just didn't want to, and that was that.

We climbed up the glass stairs. We could see everything beneath us as plainly as on the palm of the hand.

You who are reading these notes, whoever you

may be, at least you have a sun overhead. And if you were ever as ill as I was then, you would know what the sun is like and can be like in the morning; you know that rosy, transparent, warm gold. And the air itself is slightly rosy, and everything is imbued with the gentle blood of the sun, everything is alive: and living people are smiling to the last one. And I can see something pulsating and flowing across in the glass juices of *Integral*; I can see that *Integral* is thinking about its great and terrible future, about the burdensome cargo of inescapable happiness that it will bear aloft to you, the unknown ones, you, eternally seeking and never finding. You will find, you will be happy. You are under obligation to be happy, and you have not long to wait now.

The hull of *Integral* was almost ready: an elegant, elongated ellipsoid of our glass, as everlasting as gold, as flexible as steel. I could see that they were fixing the transverse ribs to the glass hull from within: frames laterally, stringers longitudinally. They were laying the foundation for the gigantic rocket engine in the stern. Every three seconds, the mighty tail of *Integral* would eject flame and gases down into cosmic space and the ship would hurtle on and on, a fiery Tamerlane of happiness...

I could see that in conformity with Taylor, rhythmically, rapidly, in time, like the levers of a single enormous machine, the people down below were bending down, straightening up, turning round. They held shining tubes: they were using fire to cut and weld glass panels, angles, ribs and brackets. I could see the transparent glass monster-cranes gliding slowly over the glass rails, and, just like the people, obediently turning round, bending over, poking their loads into the womb of *Integral*. And they were the same: humanised, perfect people. It was the loftiest, most incredible beauty, harmony, music... I must go down to them and join them as soon as possible!

And now, shoulder to shoulder, fused with them, caught up in the steel rhythm... Measured movements: resiliency circular, ruddy cheeks; mirror-like brows unclouded by the madness of thought. I was sailing over a mirror sea. I was relaxing.

Suddenly, one of them turned placidly to me.

"So how are you? Is it better today?"

"Is what better?"

"But look, you weren't here yesterday. We thought you were in some kind of danger..."

His brow was beaming, his smile was childlike and innocent.

The blood rushed to my face. I could not, no, I could not lie to those eyes. I said nothing, I was drowning...

Above, a porcelain face beaming with round whiteness pushed itself into the hatch.

"Hey, D-503! Kindly come here! We've got a stiff frame with the cantilevers and the nodal moments are giving stress on the square."

I didn't wait till he finished, I rushed up the ladder to him, ignominiously saving myself by flight. I hadn't the strength to raise my eyes—I had spots in front of them from the glittering glass steps under my feet, and with each step it was even more hopeless: there was no place for me, a criminal, a poisoned man. Never again was I to merge with the exact mechanical rhythm or float over the mirror-placid sea. I am to roast eternally, wander to and fro, seek for a corner where I could hide my eyes—eternally, until I finally found the strength to come through and...

A spark of ice pierced me through and through: I didn't matter, I made no difference, but I must think of her too, and she too is to...

I climbed out of the hatch on to the deck and stopped. I didn't know where to go now, I didn't know why I had come here. I looked up. Enervated by noon, the sun was dimly climbing up the sky. Below was *Integral*, all grey glass and inert. Rose-red blood was flowing out, and it was clear to me that all this was only my fantasy, that everything was as it had been before, and yet it was still clear to me that...

"What are you doing, D-503? Have you gone deaf? I've been calling and calling you... What's the matter?" It was the Second Constructor, right in my ear. He must have been shouting for some time.

What was the matter with me? I had let go of the controls. The engine was roaring away, the aero was shuddering and racing onwards, but it was out of control and I didn't know where I was heading for so fast: down, to crash on to the ground, or up, into the sun, into the fire...

YELLOW. THE TWO-DIMENSIONAL SHADOW.
THE INCURABLE SOUL.

I haven't made any entries for several days, I don't know how many. All days are the same colour—yellow, like dry, sun-baked sand, without a scrap of shade, not a drop of water, endless yellow sand. I can't live without her, and she, since she vanished so inexplicably in the Ancient House that day...

Since then, I have only seen her once on a promenade. Two, three, four days ago—I don't know. All days are as one. I had a glimpse of her, she filled my empty, yellow world for a second. Hand in hand with her, no higher than her shoulder, went the double S, and the thin paper doctor, and a fourth man—I can only remember his fingers: uncommonly thin, white and long, they flowed out of his unifa sleeves like rays of light. She raised her hand and waved to me; she bent across to the one with the ray-fingers. I caught the word "Integral". All four glanced at me and then were instantly lost in the grey-blue sky, and again that yellow, parched road.

That evening, she had a rose ticket for me. I stood in front of the numerator and implored it with tenderness and hatred to click so that "I-330" would appear in the white gap. The door kept slamming, out of the lift walked pale ones, tall ones, rosy ones, dark ones; blinds were falling all round. But she wasn't there. She didn't come.

And perhaps just at that moment, at exactly 22, as I am writing this, she is leaning her shoulder against someone with her eyes closed and is saying to that someone, "Do you love me?" To whom is she saying it? Who is he? The one with the ray-fingers, or the fat-lipped, spluttering R? Or S?

S... Why do I hear his flat, slapping footsteps behind me all the time, as if he were crossing puddles? Why does he follow me like a shadow every day? In front, to one side, from behind, a grey-blue, two-dimensional shadow: people walk through it and step on it, but it's still always there, close to me, attached to me by an invisible umbilical cord. Is she that umbilical cord? I don't know. Or perhaps the Guardians already know that I...

If you were told that your shadow sees you, sees you all the time, would you understand? Suddenly, I have a strange sensation: my hands are not my own, they are hampering me. I find myself marching out of step and waving my arms. Or suddenly I must look round, but I can't look round however hard I try—my neck is shackled. And I flee, I flee faster and faster. And I can feel with my back that the shadow is running faster behind me too, and there is no getting away from it, no getting away from it at all...

At last I'm alone in my room. But now there's something else: the telephone. I pick up the receiver again. "Yes, I-330, please." And again in the earpiece a slight noise, someone's footsteps going along the corridor past the doors of her room, and silence... I slam down the receiver and cannot stand it any longer. I must go there and see her.

That was yesterday. I hurried over there and for a whole hour, from 16 to 17, I wandered about near the house in which she lives. The numbers were marching past me in formation. Thousands of feet were tramping in time; a million-legged Leviathan was lurching past. But I alone, cast up by a storm on to a desert island, am looking and looking for something in the grey-blue billows.

At any moment now, the sharply mocking angle of eyebrows tilted towards the temples and the dark windows of eyes will appear from somewhere, and there, within, a fireplace is ablaze, people's shadows are moving about. And I shall go in there, inside, and I shall say, "You know I can't live without you. So why be like this?"

But she is silent. I suddenly hear the silence, I suddenly hear the Music Factory, and I understand: it is already after 17, all have long since left, I am alone, I am late. Around me lies a glass desert flooded with yellow sunlight. Shining walls hang upside-down on the glassy surface, as on water, and I too am ridiculously suspended upside-down.

I must, as soon as possible, this very minute, obtain a certificate in the Medical Bureau to the effect that I am ill, otherwise I'll be arrested and— — But perhaps that would be the best thing. To stay here and wait calmly until they notice and consign me to the Operating Theatre—it would put an end to it all, it would atone for everything.

A slight rustle and a S-shaped shade in front of me. Without looking, I felt two steely grey gimlets drilling rapidly into me, so I smiled for all I was worth and said—I had to say something:

"I ... I have to get to the Medical Bureau."

"What's the trouble? What are you standing here for?"

Stupidly inverted, hanging by the feet, I did not speak, flushing all over with shame.

"Follow me," said S sternly.

I went meekly, waving unnecessary arms that did not belong to me. I couldn't raise my eyes, I walked along all the time in a weird, upside-down world. I could see machines bottom-up and people with their feet fixed antipodes-wise to the ceiling and, still lower down, the sky fused with the thick glass of the roadway. I remember that the most hurtful thing of all was that for the last time in my life I had seen all this inverted and unreal. But I could not raise my eyes.

We stopped. There were steps in front of me. When I mounted the first, I saw figures in white doctors' overalls and the enormous mute Bell...

With an effort, as if by a helical drive, I finally tore my eyes away from the glass under my feet and suddenly the gold letters of "Medical" splashed into my face... I didn't even think about why he had brought me here and not to the Operating Theatre or why he had spared me. I cleared the steps in a single bound, slammed the door behind me, and gasped for air. As if I had not breathed since morning, as if my heart had not been beating and only now could I breathe for the first time; only now did the sluices open in my chest.

Two men. One, squat and fat-legged, was tossing the patients on to the horns of his eyes; the other was incredibly thin, with gleaming scissor-lips and a knife-blade nose... The same one.

I rushed to him as if he was my own kin, straight on to the blade, and said something about insomnia, dreams, shadows, a yellow world. The scissor-lips were flashing and smiling.

"You're in a bad way. You've evidently developed a soul."

A soul? That strange, ancient, long-forgotten word. We sometimes used to say "soul to soul", "soullessly" and "soul-destroying", but soul— —

"That's ... that's very dangerous," I babbled.

"Incurable," chopped the scissors.

"But... what's it all about, exactly? I somehow can't... I can't imagine..."

"Look ... how am I to put it... You're a mathematician, aren't you, after all?"

"Yes."

"Well, it's like this: a plane, a surface, this mirror, say. On the surface you and I, as you can see, are screwing up our eyes against the sun, and this blue electric spark in the tube, and see, the shadow of an aero just flitted past. Only on the surface, only for a second. But imagine this: because of some kind of fire, this impenetrable surface suddenly softens and nothing glides over it

97

any more—everything penetrates inside, into that mirror world that, out of curiosity, we used to stare into when we were children—children are not at all so stupid, let me assure you. The plane has become a volume, a body, a world, and all this inside the mirror is inside you—the sun, and the slipstream from the aero propeller, and your trembling lips, and someone else's lips too. And the cold mirror reflects, you see, it throws back; but this absorbs, and everything leaves a trace that endures forever. Once a scarcely noticeable wrinkle on someone's face, and it is in you forever; once you've heard a drop fail in the silence, you can hear it now..."

"Yes, yes, precisely..." I gripped him by the arm. "I heard it just now: drops are slowly dripping from the washbasin tap into the silence. And I knew that this was forever. But even so, why a soul all of a sudden? It wasn't there before, it just wasn't, and now, suddenly... Why has no one else got one, and yet I..."

I dug my fingers even harder into the incredibly thin arm: it was an uncanny feeling, losing one's lifebelt.

"Why? And why haven't we got feathers and wings? Why we only got shoulder-blades, the foundations for wings? Because we don't need wings any more; we have the aero, and wings would only get in the way. Wings are for flying, but there is nowhere for us to fly to any more: we have arrived, we have found. Isn't that so?"

I nodded in embarrassment. He looked at me and laughed sharply, like a stroke of the lancet.

The other man heard, clumped in heavy-footed from his office and, with his eyes, tossed my incredibly thin doctor on to his horns and did the same to me.

"What's all this about? The soul? The soul, you say? How stupid! That way we'll all end up with cholera. I've told you (tossing the incredibly thin one on to his horns), I've told you: everybody's fantasy must be extirpated. Only surgery can help here, nothing but surgery..."

He donned an enormous pair of X-ray spectacles, walked round for a long time peering through the bones of the skull into my brain and wrote something down in a book.

"Very interesting, very! Listen, would you agree to being ... put down in spirit? For the Unified State, it would be extremely ... it would help us to avert an epidemic... If, of course, you have no special grounds..."

"Yes, but you see," said the thin one, "Number D-503 is the constructor of *Integral*, and I am convinced that this would damage..."

"A-a-ah," mumbled the other, and he stomped back into his office.

We were left alone together. The paper hand lightly and affectionately lay on my arm, the profile face bent over close to me, and he whispered:

"But I'll tell you a secret: you're not the only one who has it. My colleague is right when he talks about an epidemic. Try and remember—haven't you yourself noticed anyone with the same thing, very similar, very close?.." and he looked at me intently. At what was he hinting, or at whom? Could it be...

"Listen..." I jumped up off my chair. But he had already started talking loudly about something else.

"...As for your insomnia and dreams, let me give you one piece of advice: go for walks more often. Get started tomorrow morning, even if it's only to the Ancient House."

Smiling subtly, he drilled me with his eyes again. And it seemed to me that I had clearly seen a word wrapped in the fine fabric of that smile—a letter, a name, a single name... Or was it only fantasy again?

I could hardly wait for him to write me a medical certificate for today and tomorrow. Then, once again, I shook his hand without saying a word and hurried outside.

My heart was as light and swift as an aero, and it was bearing me higher and higher. I knew that tomorrow there would be some kind of joy. But what precisely?

Entry No. 17
Summary:
THROUGH GLASS. I DIE. CORRIDORS.

I am completely bewildered. Yesterday, at the very moment when I was thinking that everything had now been disentangled and all the x's had been found, new unknowns appeared in my equation.

The beginning of the coordinates in all this story was, of course, the Ancient House. From that point ran the x-axis, the y-axis and the z-axis, on which, since recently, my whole world had been constructed. I was walking towards the beginning of the coordinates along the x-axis (59th Prospekt). All of yesterday was like a multicoloured whirlwind inside me: inverted houses and people, agonisingly alien hands, gleaming scissors, water dripping urgently from the tap—it had been like that, it had been like that once. And all this, tearing the flesh apart, was spinning wildly round and round where the "soul" is, behind the fire-molten surface.

To follow the doctor's recommendation, I deliberately chose a route not along the hypotenuse, but along the catheti of the triangle. And now here was the second cathetus-the circular road at the foot of the Green Wall. From the boundless green ocean behind the Wall there came rolling at me a wild billow of roots, flowers, branches, leaves, rearing up as if it would lash me at any moment and I would be changed from a human being, the most refined and subtle of mechanisms, into...

Fortunately, the glass of the Wall stood between me and that wild green ocean. O great, divinely limiting wisdom of walls, of barriers! Perhaps this is the greatest of all inventions. Man ceased to be a wild animal only when he built the first wall. Man ceased to be a wild man only when we built the Green Wall, with which we insulated our mechanical, perfect world from the irrational, disorderly world of trees, birds, animals...

I could see watching me as in a mist and blurred through the glass, the blunt muzzle of a beast and two yellow eyes stubbornly repeating a thought that was incomprehensible to me. We looked for a long time into one another's eyes, down those shafts from the superficial world into that other world below the surface. And the thought stirred in me, "Supposing that yellow-eyed creature, in its ugly, dirty pile of leaves and its un-calculated life, is happier than we are?"

I waved my hand. The yellow eyes blinked, re-ceded, vanished into the foliage. What a wretched creature! What an absurdity! It's happier than us! Perhaps happier than I am—yes. But after all, I'm only an exception, I'm sick.

And I, too... I could already see the dark red walls of the Ancient House, and the dear old woman's hairy mouth, and I rushed towards her as fast as my legs could carry me.

"Is she here?"

The skin-covered mouth opened slowly.

"And who might she be?"

"Who indeed? I-330, of course!.. We were to-gether that time, on the aero..."

"Ah, yes, yes... Yes, yes, yes..."

Ray-wrinkles round the lips, crafty rays from the yellow eyes penetrating more and more deeply into me... Finally:

"Very well, then... She's here, she came through not long ago."

She was here. I saw a bush of silvery-bitter wormwood at the old woman's feet (the courtyard of the Ancient House was part of the museum, it had been carefully preserved in its prehistoric form); the wormwood stretched out a branch to the old woman's hand and she stroked it, and there was a yellow band of sunlight on her knees. And for a single moment, the sun, the old woman and the yellow eyes were all one, we were firmly bound together by veins of some kind, and along those veins flowed the same common, turbulent and magnificent blood...

I feel ashamed to write about this now, but I promised in these notes to be absolutely frank. Well, I bent down and I kissed that skin-covered, soft, mossy mouth. The old woman wiped it and laughed...

I ran through the familiar, half-cramped, echoing rooms and straight into the bedroom, for some reason. I had only just seized the door-handle, when it suddenly struck me, "But what if she isn't alone in there?" I stopped and listened. But all I could hear was the thudding—not inside me, but somewhere near me—of my heart.

I went in. The wide, uncrumpled bed. The mirror. The other mirror on the wardrobe door, and, in the keyhole, the key on its ancient ring. But no one to be seen.

I called softly:

"Are you here?" And even more softly, with my eyes closed, and scarcely breathing, just as if I was down on my knees before her, "My darling!"

Silence. Only the water dripping hastily from the tap into the white sink of the washstand. I can't explain why now, but I found that alone unpleasant. I firmly tightened the tap and went out. She was clearly not there. Which meant she was in some other "flat".

I ran down the broad, gloomy staircase and tried to open first one door, then a second, then a third. Locked. Everything was locked, except for "our" flat, and there was nobody in there.

And yet I went back there again, I don't even know why myself. I walked slowly, with an effort; the soles of my shoes were suddenly cast-iron. I distinctly remember thinking, "It's an error that the force of gravity is a constant. Consequently, all my formulae..."

Suddenly, an explosion. Right down below, a door slammed and someone stepped quickly over the tiles. I was light and superlight again. I rushed to the banisters to bend over and cry out everything in one word, in one shout, "You!"

And I froze. Down below, its pink ear-wings flapping, the head of S was gliding along, painted into the dark square of shadow from the window sash.

A single, stark, lightning conclusion, without premises (I don't know the premises, not even to this day): "He mustn't see me, not on any account."

On tiptoe, hugging the wall, I slipped upstairs to that unlocked flat.

I stood for a second at the door. He was clumping upstairs and he was coming this way! As long as the door didn't creak! I implored that door, but it was wooden: it creaked and whined. Like a whirlwind, green, red and the yellow Buddha shot past and I was in front of the mirror-door of the wardrobe: my pale face, my listening eyes, my lips... Through the noise of my blood I could hear the creaking of the door. It was he, he.

I clutched at the key to the wardrobe door and the ring swayed. It reminded me of something, and again there was a stark, instant conclusion without premises, or, to be more precise, there was the fragment of a conclusion: "At that time— —". I quickly opened the wardrobe door—I was inside, in the dark, I shut it tight. One step and the floor rocked under my feet. Slowly and softly I began gliding downwards, everything went dark in front of my eyes and I died.

* * *

Later, when I wrote down all these strange events, I ransacked my memory and consulted books, and now, of course, I understand: it had been a state of temporary death, known to the ancients and, to the best of my knowledge, completely unfamiliar to us.

I have no idea how long I was dead; most likely for about five to ten seconds in all, but only after a certain time did I return from the dead and open my eyes. It was dark, and I could feel myself sinking down and down... I reached out my hand and clutched—and was scratched by a rough, rapidly moving wall. There was blood on my finger. Clearly, this was not a trick of my morbid imagination. But what was it, then?

I could hear my spasmodic, tremulous breathing (I am ashamed to admit it, all this was so unexpected and incomprehensible). One minute, two, three—and downwards all the time. Finally, a light bump. What had been falling under my feet was now motionless. I fumbled about in the dark and found a kind of handle, I pushed, a door opened, and there was a dim light. I could see behind me a small square platform rising swiftly upwards. I rushed back, but it was already too late: I was marooned, cut off down here... I didn't know where "here" was.

A corridor. A one-thousand-ton silence. On the round vaults, electric light bulbs, an endless, glittering, trembling dotted line. Somewhat like the "tubes" of our own underground tunnels, but much narrower and not built of our glass, but some other ancient material. A thought flashed through my mind about the cellars in which people are supposed to have taken refuge during the Two Hundred Years War... It made no difference: I had to keep walking.

I suppose I must have carried on for about twenty minutes. I turned right; the corridor was wider and the bulbs were brighter. There was a kind of confused roar. Perhaps machines, perhaps voices, I didn't know, but I was beside a heavy, opaque door. The noise was coming from behind it.

I knocked once, then again, more loudly. The

noise died down behind the door. Something clanged and, slowly, heavily, the door swung open.

I don't know which of the two of us was more stupefied. In front of me was my blade-nosed, incredibly thin doctor.

"You? Here?" His scissors closed with a snap. As for me, I might never have known a single human word. I said nothing, just stared, and simply could not understand what he was telling me. Perhaps that I should go away, because he then quickly pushed me with his flat paper stomach to the end of the brighter part of the corridor and gave me a shove in the back.

"Allow me ... I wanted ... I thought it was her, I-330. But I was being followed..."

"Stay here!" snapped the doctor, and he disappeared.

At last! At last she was beside me, here, and it didn't matter where "here" was. The familiar, saffron-yellow silk, the biting smile, the eyes veiled with a blind... My lips, my arms and my knees trembled, and a very silly thought came to my head:

"Vibrations are sound. A tremor should make a noise. Why is nothing audible?"

Her eyes opened for me, wide open, and I went inside them...

"I couldn't stand it any more! Where have you been? Why?.." Without taking my eyes off her for a moment, I was talking as in a fever, quickly, incoherently, perhaps even only thinking it all. "A shadow—following me... I died—out of the wardrobe... Because this man of yours ... talks with scissors: I have a soul... Incurable..."

"An incurable soul! My poor dear!" She burst out laughing, and I was sprinkled with laughter: all my delirium passed off, and suddenly sparkles of laughter were glittering and ringing everywhere, and how good everything was, how good!

The doctor came round the corner again, that miraculous, magnificent, incredibly thin doctor.

"Well?" He stopped beside her.

"It's all right, it's all right! I'll explain later. He accidentally... Say I'll be back in ... in about fifteen minutes..."

The doctor flitted round the corner. She waited. The door shut hollowly. Then slowly, slowly, ever deeper and deeper she thrust that sharp, sweet needle into my heart: she pressed against me with her shoulder, her arm, all of her, and we went off together, together—two of us as one...

I don't remember where we turned off into the darkness, and, once in the dark, up some steps, endless steps, in silence. I couldn't see her, but I knew she was walking, like me, with her eyes shut, blind, her head flung back; biting her lips—and she could hear music—my almost inaudible trembling.

I found myself in one of the countless secluded corners in the courtyard of the Ancient House: there was a kind of fence,—bare, stony ribs and the yellow teeth of ruined walls rising out of the ground. She opened her eyes and said, "The day after tomorrow at 16." She went away.

Did this really happen? I don't know. I shall

find out the day after tomorrow. There is only one real clue: the skin is torn on the fingertips of my right hand. But today, on *Integral*, the Second Constructor assured me that he had seen me accidently touch a grinding wheel with those fingers, and so that's all there is to it. Well, it may be so. It may very well be so. I don't know. I don't know anything.

Entry No. 18
Summary:

LOGICAL THICKET.
WOUNDS AND PLASTER.
NEVER AGAIN.

I lay down yesterday and promptly sank down to the drowsy bottom, like an overloaded ship that has suddenly capsized. Thickness of dense, wavering green water. And I slowly swam from the bottom upwards, and somewhere in the middle depths I opened my eyes: my room, and the still green, and chilly morning. There were splinters of sunlight on the glass mirror-door of the wardrobe and they dazzled me. This prevented me from accurately fulfilling the hours of sleep as laid down by the Tablet. It would have been best to open the wardrobe. But I was all entangled as if in a spider's web, it was covering my eyes and I hadn't the strength to get up.

I did so nevertheless, opened the door, and

suddenly, behind the mirror-door, extricating herself from her gown, all flushed, was I-330. I am so accustomed by now even to the downright incredible that as far as I can remember I wasn't even in the least surprised, asked no questions, immediately went into the wardrobe, slammed the door behind me and, gasping for breath, quickly, blindly and hungrily possessed her. I can see it as if it were happening now: through a chink in the door, in the darkness, a sharp sunbeam was refracted like a flash of lightning on the floor, on the side of the wardrobe, higher—and now that cruel, flashing blade fell on to her exposed throat... And there was something terrifying to me about this so that I couldn't bear it, screamed, and opened my eyes again.

My room. Still a green, chill morning. A splinter of sunlight on the wardrobe door. I am in bed. Asleep. But my heart is still beating violently, trembling, spurting. I have pains in my fingertips, in my knees, it undoubtedly happened. And now I don't know which was dream and which was reality: the irrational magnitudes are growing through everything durable, habitual, three-dimensional, and instead of firm, polished surfaces, everything around is twisted and shaggy...

It will be a long time before the bell rings. I lie and think, and an extremely strange logical chain begins to unwind.

In the superficial world, a curve or a body corresponds to every equation, to every formula. For irrational formulae, for my $\sqrt{-1}$ we do not know of any corresponding bodies, we have never seen them... But the horror is that although they are invisible, these bodies exist, inevitably and inescapably they must be there: because, in mathematics, the fantastic, prickly shadows of the irrational formulae pass before us as on a screen, and mathematics and death alike never make mistakes. If we do not see those bodies in our world, on the surface, for them there is, there inevitably must be, a whole enormous world down under the surface...

I jumped up without waiting for the bell and began running round the room. My mathematics, hitherto the sole stable and unshakeable island in my deranged life, had also broken away to begin floating about and whirling round and round. Did it mean that this stupid "soul" was as real as my unifa or my boots, although I could not see them just at that moment (they were behind the mirror-door of the wardrobe)? And if my boots weren't an illness, why was the "soul" an illness?

I sought and could not find a way out of that tangled logical thicket. It was as unfamiliar and weird as the tangle behind the Green Wall, and it, too, harboured weird, incomprehensible creatures that spoke without words. I dreamed that, as if through thick glass, I could see an infinitely enormous and at the same time infinitely small scorpion-like creature with a hidden yet all the time palpable minus-sting $\sqrt{-1}$... Or perhaps it was nothing other than my "soul", like the legendary scorpion of the ancients who voluntarily used to let themselves be stung to death with everything that...

The bell. Day. All that, without dying, without disappearing, was only covered by the daylight; just as visible objects, without dying, by nightfall are covered by the nocturnal dark when night falls. There was a light, wavering mist in my head. Through the mist I could see long glass tables: balloon-heads munching slowly, in silence, in rhythm. A metronome was tapping through the mist from far away, and to its familiar and affectionate music, mechanically, with all the others, I counted up to fifty: fifty legitimate masticating movements per bite. And, automatically marching to the rhythm, I went down and, like all the rest, entered my name in the book of those leaving. But I felt that I was living separately from all the others, on my own, screened off by a soft, soundproof wall, and behind that wall there was a different world...

But just one point: if that world is only mine, then why is it in these notes? What are these stupid "dreams", wardrobes and unending corridors doing in here? And I see with regret that instead of a harmonious and strictly mathematical poem in honour of the Unified State, a kind of fantastic adventure novel is working out for me. Oh, if only it really was just a novel and not my own present life, filled with x's, $\sqrt{-1}$ and lapses.

Perhaps, however, everything is for the best. Most probably of all, you, my unknown readers, are children compared with us (after all, we have been raised by the Unified State and have consequently attained the loftiest heights possible for man). And, like children, only then will you swallow without a cry all the bitter things that I shall give you when this has been carefully soused with the thick syrup of adventure...

In the evening

Do you know the feeling when you are soaring up in an aero in a blue spiral, the window is open, the wind is buffeting your face and there is no Earth, you forget about the Earth, it is as far away from you as Saturn, Jupiter or Venus? That is how I am living now, with a wind buffeting my face, and I have forgotten about the Earth, I have forgotten my dear, rosy O But the Earth still exists, sooner or later I will have to glide down on to it, and I only close my eyes before the day when her name, 0-90, will be on my Sex Table.

This evening, faraway Earth reminded me of its existence.

To carry out the doctor's prescription (I sincerely, sincerely wish to recover), I wandered for two hours along the glass, rectilinear wildernesses of the prospekts. All, in conformity with the Tablet, were in the auditoriums, and I alone... It was, indeed, an unnatural spectacle. Imagine a human finger cut off from the whole, from the hand—a separate human finger, bent over, crooked, dancing, running along a glass pavement. That finger was I. And the strangest, most unnatural thing of all was that the finger didn't in the least want to be on the hand, to be with the other fingers. It wanted to be either alone, like this, or—all right, I have nothing more to hide—or together with her,

113

with that woman, transfusing all of myself into her again through the shoulder, through the clasped fingers of the hands...

I returned home when the sun was already setting. The rosy evening ash on the glass of the walls, on the gold spire of the accumulator tower, on the voices and smiles of the numbers coming the other way. Is it not strange: the fading rays of the sun strike at exactly the same angle as the ones that catch fire in the morning, and yet everything is completely different, the rosiness is different—just now it is gentle, a tiny shade sour, but in the morning it will be resonant and sizzling again.

Downstairs, in the vestibule, U, the attendant, took out a letter from under a pile of envelopes covered with rose-red ash and handed it to me. She is, I repeat, a very respectable woman and I am convinced that her feelings for me are of the best.

And yet I feel uneasy every time I see those jowls that are as pendulous as a fish's gills.

Holding out the letter to me in a gnarled hand, U sighed. But that sigh only slightly stirred the curtain that separated me from the world. All of me was projected on to the envelope trembling in my hands. I never doubted that it was from I-330.

At this point came a second sigh, so obviously underlined twice, that I tore myself away from the envelope and saw, between the gills, through the bashful jalousies of the lowered eyes, a tender, all-enveloping, dazzling smile. And then:

"Poor you, poor you," and a sigh underlined three times, and a scarcely discernible nod at the

114

letter (she naturally, in the line of duty, knew its contents).

"But really, I... But why?"

"No, no, my dear, I know you better than you know yourself. I've been watching you closely for some time, and I can see that you need to walk hand in hand through life with someone who has studied life for many years..."

I felt plastered all over by her smile: it was the dressing on the wounds which the letter trembling in my hands was about to inflict on me. Finally, very softly through the modest jalousies:

"I'll think, my dear, I'll think. And rest assured, if I feel I have strength enough—no, no, I must think it over first..."

Great Benefactor! Am I really destined... Does she really mean to say that— —

Ripples in front of my eyes, thousands of sine waves, the letter dances. I go nearer to the light, to the wall. The sun is fainter there, and from there—the dark-rose, sad ash falls ever more thickly on to me, on to the floor, on to my hands, on to the letter.

The envelope is torn open—find the signature as quickly as possible—and a wound: it isn't I-330, it's O. And another wound: in the right-hand corner at the bottom of the page, there's an ink-blot—a drop of something has fallen on to it... I cannot bear blots: it doesn't matter whether they're made by ink or by... But I know that previously I would have simply found it unpleasant, my eyes would have found it unpleasant as a result of that unpleasant blob. But why is that little grey smudge like a cloud this time, and why has everything become more leaden and more dark as a result? Or is it the "soul" again?

The Letter:

"You know ... or perhaps, you don't know—I can't write properly, but it doesn't matter: you now know that without you there won't be a single day for me, a single morning, a single spring. Because to me R is only ... but that's not important to you. I am very grateful to him anyway: had I been without him these last few days, I just don't know what... I've lived through ten or perhaps twenty years during these last few days and nights. As if my room wasn't rectangular, but round, and with no end—around and around it, all one and the same thing, and no doors anywhere.

"I can't live without you because I love you. Because I see and understand that you need no one in this world now, no one at all except for that other one, and, you see, it is precisely because I love you that I must— —

"I only need another two or three days to piece together something more or less like the former 0-90 out of myself, and I shall go and personally make a statement to the effect that I am cancelling my request for you, and that should make it better for you, that should make it good. I shall never bother you again. Please forgive me.

"O."

Never again. Of course, it would be better that way: she was right. But why, why?..

116

AN INFINITELY SMALL MAGNITUDE OF THE THIRD ORDER. FROM UNDER THE BROWS. OVER THE BALUSTRADE.

Over there, in the strange corridor with the trembling dotted line of dull lamp bulbs ... or no, no, not there: later, when we were together in a secluded corner in the courtyard of the Ancient House, she said, "The day after tomorrow." That "day after tomorrow" was today, and everything was on wings, the day was flying and our *Integral* was already winged: they had finished fitting the rocket engine and were trying it out today as a bench test. What magnificent, mighty salvoes, and to me, each of them was a salute in honour of that one and only person, in honour of today.

At the first blast (= shot), something like ten careless numbers from our shipyard happened to be under the nozzle and absolutely nothing was left of them but crumbs and soot. I record with pride here that the rhythm of our work never faltered for a second because of that, no one quailed, and we and our machine-tools continued our rectilinear and circular movements with the same precision as if nothing had happened. Ten numbers would hardly be a hundred-millionth part of the mass of the Unified State, and in practical calculations that is an infinitely small magnitude of the third order. Arithmetically illiterate pity was only known to the ancients: we find it funny.

And I find it funny that yesterday I could start thinking, and even write on these pages, about a pathetic little grey stain, or blot. It's all the same "softening of the surface", which ought to be diamond hard, like our walls (the ancient saying: "Like peas against a wall").

Sixteen hours. I have not been out on the supplementary promenade. Who knows? Perhaps she might think of coming right now, when everything is ringing in the sunshine...

I am almost alone in the house. Through the sun-soaked walls I can see far to the right, to the left and downwards—rooms suspended in mid-air, empty, duplicating one another as in mirrors. Except that a thin shadow is gliding slowly up the pale-blue staircase that is very faintly outlined by the sun. Now I can hear footsteps, and I can see and feel through the door: a sticking-plaster smile on my lips—and then the footsteps go past me and down another staircase...

The numerator clicks. I throw the whole of myself into the narrow white gap and ... and it's an unfamiliar male number. The lift booms and slams. In front of me is a brow carelessly and lopsidedly pulled down over the eyes... As for those eyes, I have the very strange impression that he is speaking from there, from under the brows where the eyes are.

"A letter from her to you ... (from under the eyebrows, from under the awning). She asks you to do, without fail, everything she says."

A glance round from under the eyebrows, from under the awning. No, there's no one else here, no one else at all, so come on! After another glance round, he shoves the envelope at me and goes out. I am alone.

No, not alone. A rose ticket comes out of the envelope and the scarcely perceptible fragrance of her. It is she, she is coming, she is coming to me. I take out the letter to read it with my own eyes, to make myself absolutely certain...

What? Impossible! I read it again, skipping whole lines: "Ticket... and be sure to lower the blinds as if I was really with you... It is vital to me that they should think that I... I am very, very sorry..."

I tear the letter to pieces. I glance in the mirror for a second: the reflection of my distorted, broken eyebrows. I pick up the ticket to deal with it as with her note...

"She asks you to do, without fail, everything she says."

My hands weaken and loosen their grip. The ticket falls on to the table. She's stronger than me and I will obviously do as she wants. And yet ... and yet, I don't know. We shall see. Evening is a long way off... The ticket is lying on the table.

I can see my distorted, broken eyebrows in the mirror. Why couldn't I have a doctor's certificate for today too? I could go and walk, walk endlessly, right round the Green Wall, and then collapse into bed, on to the bottom... But I must be in Auditorium No. 13, I must screw myself up tight for two hours, two hours without moving, when I need to shout and stamp my feet.

The lecture. Very strange that it wasn't a metallic voice coming from the glittering apparatus as usual, but one that seemed soft, shaggy and mossy. A woman's voice. In my imagination, she looked the way a bent little old woman might, like the one at the Ancient House.

The Ancient House... And it all suddenly shot up like a fountain from below, and I had to screw myself up with all my strength in order not to drown the whole auditorium with a scream. Soft, furry words going through me, and all that was left of them was something about children, about child-breeding. I was like a photographic plate: I was printing everything inside myself with a kind of alien, outside, meaningless exactitude: a gold sickle—the glitter of light on the loudspeaker; under it a child, a living demonstration, was reaching for the heart; the hem of the tiny unifa was thrust into its mouth; the tiny fist was clenched, the thumb was pushed into it—a light, puffy shadow-fold on the wrist. Like a photographic plate, I printed it: now there was a naked leg, now it swung over the edge, the rosy fan of the toes was stepping on to the air—at any moment now, the baby would fall on to the floor— —

And a woman screamed, a unifa flapped transparent wings on to the stage and she snatched up the child, planting her lips on to the puffy fold on

120

the wrist, shifted it to the middle of the table and came down from the stage. It was printed out in me: a rosy crescent of a mouth with the horns pointing downwards, dark-blue saucer eyes filled to the brim. It was O. And, as when reading a harmonious formula, I suddenly felt the necessity, the legitimacy of this trivial incident.

She sat down just behind me, to the left. I looked round. She obediently took her eyes off the table with the child and trained her eyes on me, into me, and again she, I and the table on the stage—three points, and lines were drawn through those points, the projections of inevitable and not yet visible events.

Homewards along the street that was green in the dusk and already big-eyed with lights. I could hear myself ticking all the time like a watch. And the hands within me would move across a number at any moment and I would do something irrevocable. It was necessary to I-330 that someone there should think she was at my place. But she was necessary to me, and what did her "necessary" mean to me? I didn't want to be someone else's blinds—I didn't want to, and that was that.

The familiar footsteps were slapping behind me as if through puddles. I didn't look round, I knew who it was: S. He would follow me as far as the door and would then probably stand below on the pavement and drill with his eyes all the way up into my room until the blinds fell, concealing someone else's crime... He, the Guardian Angel, had put an end to it. I decided against it. I made up my mind.

When I went up to my room and turned the switch, I couldn't believe my eyes. O was standing near me. Or rather she was hanging there like an empty, discarded dress, and she did not seem to have a single spring under it, her arms and legs were unsprung and she spoke with an unsprung, hanging voice.

"I'm here about my letter. Did you get it? Yes? I must know your answer, I must know today."

I shrugged my shoulders. With pleasure, as if she was to blame for everything, I looked at her blue, brimful eyes, and I delayed my answer. And, with pleasure, putting the words into her one at a time, I said:

"Answer? Why, you're right. Absolutely. About everything."

"So that means... (She smiled to mask a fine tremor, but I could see it.) Very well, then! I shall—I shall go now."

And she hung over the table. Drooping eyes, legs, arms. That other one's crumpled rose ticket was still lying on the table-top. I quickly opened this manuscript of mine, "WE", and hid the ticket with it (perhaps from myself rather than from O).

"See, I keep on writing. A hundred and seventy pages already... It's turning out to be quite unexpected..."

Hers was the ghost of a voice:

"Do you remember... On page seven at the time... I made a blot, and you..."

Blue saucer eyes brimming over, soundless, hasty teardrops—down the cheeks, and the hasty words brimming over:

"I can't bear it, I shall go at once... I shan't ever bother you again, so that will be that. Only I want—I must have a child by you-leave me a child, and I'll go away, I'll go away!"

I could see that she was trembling all over under her unifa, and I felt that I too might begin trembling at any moment... I put my hands behind my back and smiled.

"What? Do you want to try the Benefactor's Machine?"

And words at me, like water brimming over a dam:

"What of it? But I'll feel it, I'll feel it inside me. And even if it's only for a few days... Just once, just once to see that fold on its wrist, the way it was back there on the table. Even if only for one day!"

Three points: she, I, and there, on the table, a tiny fist with a puffy fold.

Once in my childhood, I remember, we were taken up the accumulator tower. On the very top flight I bent over the glass balustrade; there were dots of people below, and my heart ticked sweetly: "But what if?" I held on even tighter to the handrail then; but this time I jumped down.

"Is that what you want? Fully aware that..."

Eyes closed as if turned to the sun. A damp, radiant smile.

123

"Yes, yes! That's what I want!"

I pulled the pink ticket—the other one's—out from under the manuscript and ran downstairs to the duty officer. O had seized me by the arm and screamed something, but only when I returned did I understand what. She was sitting on the edge of the bed, her hands squeezed tight between her knees.

"Was that... was that her ticket?"

"As if it matters. All right, yes, it was hers."

Something crunched. Or rather O simply stirred. She was sitting with her hands between her knees, saying nothing.

"Well? Quick..." I gripped her hand roughly and red patches (tomorrow's bruises) appeared on her wrist where there was a puffy childish fold.

That was the last thing. Then the switch was turned off, thoughts went out, darkness, sparks—and I leapt over the balustrade and plunged downwards...

Entry No. 20
Summary:

DISCHARGE.
THE MATERIAL OF IDEAS.
THE ZERO CLIFF.

A discharge is the most appropriate definition. I now see that it was just like an electric discharge. The pulse of my last few days was becoming drier, more frequent, more tense; the poles were drawing closer and closer together—a dry crackling, another millimetre—an explosion, then silence.

I'm now very quiet and empty inside, as in a house when all have left, you're lying ill in there on your own and you can hear the distinct metallic clicking of your thoughts.

Perhaps that "discharge" cured me, at last, of my tormenting "soul" and I became like the rest of us again. At least I can now, in my mind's eye, without any pain, see O on the steps of the Cube, I can see her in the Gas Bell. And if she should call out my name there, in the Operating Theatre, let her do so: in my last moments I shall reverently and gratefully kiss the punitive hand of the Benefactor. In relation to the Unified State, I have the right to bear punishment and I shall not surrender that right. Not one of us numbers ought, or dares, to refuse that right which is all the more precious because it is the only one.

...My thoughts tick softly, with metallic distinctness; the unknown aero bears me away into the blue heights of my beloved abstractions. And I can see how here, in the purest rarified air, with a light pop, like a pneumatic tyre, my reasoning about the "effective right" bursts. And I can clearly see that this is only a throwback to the stupid prejudice of the ancients, their notion of "right".

There are ideas of clay and there are ideas moulded forever in gold or our own precious glass. To test the material of an idea, all that's needed is to drop strong acid on to it. The ancients knew one such acid: *reductio ad finem*. That, apparently, was what they called it; but they feared that poison, they preferred to see at least some kind of sky, even though of clay, even though a toy, rather than a blue nothing. We, however, are adults, all praise to the Benefactor, and we have no need of toys.

Supposing we drop some acid on the idea of "right". Even among the ancients, the more mature adults knew that the source of right is force: right is a function of force. And so here we have the two pans of the scales: on one a gram, on the other a ton, on the one—the "ego", on the other—"We", the Unified State. Is it not clear that to allow the "I's" to enjoy certain rights in relation to the state and to allow the gram to balance the ton is exactly the same thing. Hence, distribution: rights to the ton and obligations to the gram; and the natural way from nonentity to greatness is to forget that you are a gram and to feel yourself as the millionth part of a ton...

You fat-bodied, rosy Venusians, you Uranians, grimy as blacksmiths, I can hear your murmurings in my dark-blue silence. But try to understand me: everything great is simple; please understand me: only the four rules of arithmetic are unshakeable and eternal. And only a morality built on those four rules shall remain great, unshakeable and eternal. That is the ultimate wisdom, that is the apex of the pyramid up which people have been scrambling for centuries, red with perspiration, kicking and gasping for breath. And from that summit—down there on the bottom, where something that has survived in us from the savagery of our forbears is still seething like a mass of worms,—from that summit, all are equal: O, the illegal mother, and the murderer, and that madman who dared to fling his verses at the Unified State. And for them, the sentence is the same: premature death. This is the divine justice of which the stone-house people dreamed, illumined by the naive and rosy rays of the dawn of history. Their "God" punished blasphemy against the Holy Church just as if it were murder.

You Uranians, stern and dark as the ancient Spaniards who were wisely able to burn at the stake, you are silent, so it seems to me that you are with me. But I can hear amongst you, rosy Venusians, something about tortures, executions and the return to barbarian times. My dears, I pity you, for you are incapable of philosophico-mathematical thought.

Human history spirals upwards, like an aero. The circles vary from gold to blood-red, but they are all equally divided into 360 degrees. And so from zero we go forward: 10, 20, 200, 360 degrees, which is back to zero again. Yes, we have indeed returned to zero. But to my mathematically thinking mind, it is clear that this zero is something different, something new. We started out to the right from zero and we have returned to zero from the left; and so, instead of plus zero, we have minus zero. D'you understand me?

I see this Zero as a kind of cliff, silent, enormous, narrow and sharp as a knife. Holding our breath in the wild and shaggy darkness, we have cast off from the black nocturnal side of the Zero

Cliff. For centuries, we have sailed like Columbuses on and on, we have circumnavigated the whole world and finally, hurrah!—fire a salute and all hands aloft. Before us is another and hitherto unknown side of the Zero Cliff, lit by the polar radiance of the Unified State, a pale-blue mass, sparks of the rainbow, suns, hundreds of suns, billions of rainbows...

What does it matter if we are only separated from the other side of the Zero Cliff by the thickness of a knife-blade? A knife is the most durable, most immortal, most inspired of all things created by man. The knife has been a guillotine, the knife has been a universal means of cutting all knots, and the way of paradoxes goes along a knife-blade—the only way worthy of the fearless mind...

Entry No. 21
Summary:

THE AUTHOR'S DUTY.
THE ICE SWELLS.
THE MOST DIFFICULT LOVE.

It was her day yesterday, but again she didn't come and again she sent an incoherent note that explained nothing. But I am calm, perfectly calm. If, notwithstanding, I behave as dictated in the note, if, notwithstanding, I take her ticket to the duty officer and then, after lowering the blinds, sit alone in my room, it is not because I hadn't the strength to go against her wishes. Amusing? Of course not! It's just that once I'm separate from all the healing plaster smiles, I can calmly write these very pages, that's the first thing. And the second: in her, in I-330, I am afraid of perhaps losing the only clue to the disclosure of all the unknowns (the business with the wardrobe, my temporary death and so on). I now feel under obligation to disclose them, simply even as the author of these notes, not to mention the fact that, in general, the unknown is organically hostile to man, and *homo sapiens* is only a man in the full sense of the word when there are no question marks at all in his grammar, only exclamation marks, commas and full stops.

Guided, as it seemed to me, specifically by my duty as a writer, I took an aero today at 16 and set course for the Ancient House again. There was a strong head wind. The aero fought its way with difficulty through the dense forest of air to the whistling and thrashing of the transparent branches. The whole city below seemed like pale-blue chunks of ice. Suddenly, a cloud, a swift, glancing shadow, the ice turns leaden-hued and swells, as in spring when you are standing on the bank and waiting for it all to crack at any moment, gush forth, whirl round and begin racing along; but minute follows minute, the ice is still motionless and you yourself swell, your heart beats more and more restlessly, more and more rapidly (incidentally, why am I writing about this and where do these strange sensations come from? The

129

icebreaker doesn't exist that could crack the most transparent and durable crystal of our life...).

There was no one at the entrance to the Ancient House. I walked round and saw the old woman doorkeeper near the Green Wall. She was shading her eyes and staring upwards. Over there, above the Wall, were the sharp black triangles of birds. They were cawing as they swooped down to attack, beating their breasts against the tough screen of electric waves, then back again, then above the Wall again.

I could see slanting, quick shadows across the wrinkled face and a quick glance at me.

"There's no one here, no one, no one! And there's nothing to go for. Nothing..."

What did she mean, nothing to go for? And what strange trick was this, to treat me merely as someone's shadow? Perhaps you yourselves are all my shadows. Have I not populated these pages with you, pages that until recently were rectangular white deserts? Without me, would you have been seen by all those whom I shall lead down the narrow paths of the lines?

I didn't say all this to her, of course. I know from personal experience that the most agonising thing of all is to raise doubts of a person's own reality, to suggest that that person is not a three-dimensional reality, but a reality of some other kind. However, all I did was to point out to her drily that it was her job to open the door. She let me into the yard.

Empty. Quiet. The wind on the other side, behind the walls, was remote, as on the day when, shoulder to shoulder, two as one, we walked up from below, out of the corridors—if only that was real. I was walking under stone arches and my footsteps were hitting the damp vaults and falling down behind me, as if someone else was following on my heels all the time. The yellow walls with their red brick pustules watched me through the dark square spectacles of windows and followed me as I opened the singing doors of barns and looked into corners, blind alleys, nooks and crannies. A wicker gate in the wall and a waste-lot—the memorial to the Great Two Hundred Years War: bare stone ribs rising from the ground, the grinning yellow jawbones of walls, an ancient stove with its vertical chimney—a ship turned to stone for eternity amid the stony yellow and red splashes of the brickwork.

I thought I had seen those yellow teeth once before, dimly, as on the bottom, through deep water, and I began searching. I stumbled into holes, tripped over stones, rusty paws clutched at my unifa and acrid, salty beads of sweat trickled down my forehead and ran into my eyes...

Nowhere! I could not find that exit from the corridors below. So much the better: it was more credible that this had all just been one of my silly "dreams".

Weary, covered all over with cobwebs and dust, I had already opened the gate to go back into the main yard when suddenly I heard a rustle and slapping footsteps behind me, and I found myself confronted by the rosy wing-ears and the double-bent smile of S.

Frowning, he screwed his gimlets into me and asked:

"Out for a stroll?"

I said nothing. My hands were in the way.

"Well, are you feeling better now?"

"Yes, thanks. I seem to be getting back to normal."

He released me, raising his eyes aloft. His head was thrown back, and for the first time I noticed his Adam's apple.

Some aeros were buzzing low above us, at about 50 metres' altitude. The slow flight and the lowered black trunks of the observation tubes told me that the Guardians were overhead. Except that there weren't two or three of them, as usual, but from ten to twelve (unfortunately, I must confine myself to approximate figures).

"Why are there so many of them today?" I had the temerity to ask.

"Why? Hm... A genuine doctor begins treating the still healthy person who will not fall ill until tomorrow, the day after tomorrow, in a week's time. Prophylaxis!"

He nodded and slapped off over the flagstones in the yard. Then he looked round and said to me over his shoulder:

"Be careful!"

I was on my own. Quiet. Empty. The birds and the wind were flying restlessly far away over the Green Wall. What had he meant by that?

The aero glided smoothly along with the current. The light, the heavy shadows of clouds; below, pale-blue domes, cubes of ice-like glass—they were turning leaden-hued, swelling...

In the evening:

I have opened my manuscript to enter on these pages a few, as it seems to me, useful (for you, my readers) thoughts about the great Day of Unanimity. That day is already near. But I now realise that I cannot write just now. All the time I am listening to the wind flapping its dark wings on the glass of the walls, all the time I keep looking round, waiting. For what? I don't know. So when the familiar rosy-brown gills appeared in my room, I was very glad, and I say this in all sincerity. She sat down, virtuously straightened the unifa fold that had fallen between her knees and quickly plastered me all over with smiles, one to each of my cracks, so that I felt pleasantly and firmly in one piece.

"You see, I arrived at the classroom today (she works at a Children's Education Factory) and there was a caricature on the wall. Yes, seriously! They'd portrayed me as a kind of fish. Perhaps I really look like..."

"No, no, really!" I hastened to say (close up, it's actually clear that there's nothing resembling gills and what I've written about them has been wholly inappropriate).

"In the final analysis, it doesn't even matter.

But it was very bad behaviour, you understand. I called the Guardians, of course. I love children very much and I consider that the most difficult and highest form of love is cruelty—you follow me?"

I should say so! It interfaced with my own thoughts. I couldn't resist it and read her an extract from my 20th entry, beginning at the point: "My thoughts tick softly, with metallic distinctness..."

Without looking, I could see the rosy-brown cheeks quivering; they moved still closer to me, and her dry, firm and even rather prickly fingers were now in mine.

"Give it, give it to me! I'll phonograph it and make the children learn it by heart. It's necessary not so much for your Venusians as for us, us—now, tomorrow, the day after tomorrow."

She looked round and, very softly:

"Have you heard? They say that on Unanimity Day..."

I jumped to my feet.

"What? What are they saying? What about Unanimity Day?"

The cosy walls no longer existed. I instantly felt as if I had been hurled outside where an enormous wind was raging over the roofs and the slanting, half-lit clouds were sinking lower and lower all the time...

U gripped me determinedly and firmly by the shoulders (although I noticed that the bones of her fingers were trembling in resonance with my agitation).

"Sit down, dear, don't get excited. People say anything... And then, if only you need it, on that day I shall be near you, I shall leave my children with someone else at the school, and I shall be with you, because you, my dear, are also a child, and you need..."

"No, no," I protested. "On no account! In that case, you really will think I'm a child and can't manage on my own... On no account!" (I must confess that I had other plans for that day.)

She smiled. The unwritten text for that smile was clearly, "Oh, what a stubborn little boy!" Then she sat down. Her eyes were downcast. Her hands were again modestly straightening the fold in her unifa that had fallen between her knees. She changed the subject.

"I think I have to make up my mind ... for your sake... No, I beseech you, don't rush me, I must do a little more thinking..."

I didn't rush her. Although I did understand that I should be happy and that there is no greater honour than to make a woman happy in the evening of her life.

...All night—wings, and I'm walking and covering my head to protect it from the wings. And then a chair. But the chair is not ours, not of the present day; it is an ancient model, made of wood. I shift my legs like a horse (right front leg and left hind leg, left front leg and right hind leg). The chair runs up to my bed and climbs on to it, and I love the wooden chair: it's uncomfortable and it hurts.

Amazing! Is it really impossible to find some means of curing that dream-sickness or making it rational, perhaps even useful?

Entry No. 22
Summary:

ARRESTED WAVES.
ALL IS PERFECTED.
I AM A MICROBE.

Imagine you are standing on the seashore. The waves are moving steadily upwards, and when they have risen, they suddenly stop, they freeze, they are arrested. It was just as unnatural when our promenade, which had been ordained by the Tablet, suddenly became confused and disorganised, then came to a halt. The last time anything like this happened, according to our chronicles, was 119 years ago, when a smoking meteorite plunged from the heavens with a whistle into the middle of the promenade.

We were walking as usual, that is, like the warriors depicted on Assyrian monuments: a thousand heads, two fused, integral legs, two integral swinging arms. At the end of the prospekt, where the accumulator tower was booming menacingly, a rectangle was coming towards us. There were guards on both sides, in front and behind; in the middle were three in unifas without their gold numbers. Everything was only too chillingly clear.

The enormous dial on the top of the tower was a face: it bent down from the clouds and, spitting out the seconds, waited indifferently. At exactly 13 hours and 6 minutes, there was a disturbance in the rectangle. It was all quite close to me, I could see the minutest details, and I vividly remember a thin, long neck and, on the temple, a tangled network of pale-blue veins like rivers on the geographical map of a small and unknown world. This unknown world was evidently a young man. He had in all probability noticed someone in our ranks, had stood on tiptoe, craned his neck and halted. One of the guards gave him a crack with the blue spark of an electric knout; he shrieked thinly, like a puppy. Then, approximately every 2 seconds, another sharp crack and another shriek.

With measured tread, like Assyrians, we marched on as before and, as I watched the elegant zigzags of sparks, I thought, "Everything in human society is being perfected without limits and ought to be perfected. What an ugly instrument the ancient knout was, and how much beauty..."

But at this point, like a bolt that flies off an engine running at full speed, the lissom, supple figure of a woman detached itself from our ranks, cried, "Enough! How dare you!" and rushed straight into the rectangle. It was like that meteor 119 years ago: the whole promenade stopped dead and our ranks were like the grey combs of waves arrested by a sudden frost.

I looked at her distantly for a second, as did everybody else: she was not a number any more, she was just a human being, she existed only as the metaphysical substance of insult inflicted on the Unified State. But after a single movement—as she turned, she swung her hips to the left—I suddenly knew that body as supple as a whiplash: my eyes knew her, my lips and my hands; at that moment I was absolutely certain of this.

Two of the guards rushed to intercept her. Now, in the still clear, mirror-point of the roadway, their trajectories would intersect and they would seize her in a moment... My heart missed a beat, then stopped, and without considering whether or not it was permissible, forbidden, absurd, sensible, I rushed straight towards that point.

I felt thousands of horror-rounded eyes on me, but this only lent even more desperately cheerful strength to the wild, hairy-handed creature that had burst out of me and was running faster and faster. I only had two paces to go when she looked round...

Before me was a quivering, freckled face and ginger eyebrows... It wasn't her! It wasn't I-330!

A wild, searing joy. I wanted to shout something like, "Come on, get her!" "Seize her!" But I could only hear myself whispering. A heavy hand was already on my shoulder and I was being held and led away. I tried explaining to them...

"Listen, you've got to understand, I thought she was..."

But how could I explain all of myself, all of my sickness as recorded on these pages? And so I simmered down and walked humbly along... A leaf torn off by a sudden gust of wind falls meekly downwards, but spins on its way, clutches at every known branch and fork and twig; so did I clutch at each of the silent sphere-heads, at the transparent ice of walls, at the golden needle of the accumulator tower poking into a cloud.

At that moment, when the dense curtain was finally ready to separate me from all that beautiful world, I saw, still in the distance, a familiar, enormous head waving rosy wing-arms and gliding over the mirror of the roadway. And a familiar flat voice was saying:

"I consider it my duty to testify that Number D-503 is sick and in no state to regulate his feelings. I am sure that he was carried away by natural indignation..."

"Yes, yes," I said, clutching at the idea. "I even shouted, 'Hold her!'"

Close behind me:

"You didn't shout anything."

"No, but I wanted to, I swear it by the Benefactor, I wanted to."

For a second, I was pierced by the grey, cold drills of eyes. I don't know whether he saw that this was (almost) the truth, or whether he had some kind of secret motive in sparing me again for a time, but he scribbled a note, handed it to one of those holding me and I was free again, that is, to be more precise, I was confined once more to the harmonious and unending Assyrian ranks.

The rectangle and, inside it, the freckled face and the temple with its geographical map of pale-blue veins disappeared round the corner, forever.

We marched on, a body with a million heads, and in each of us there was that humble joy by which molecules, atoms and phagocytes probably live. In the ancient world, as the Christians, our only (although very imperfect) predecessors, understood: humility is a virtue, but pride is a vice, and that "WE" comes from God, whereas "I" comes from the devil.

Here am I, at present in step with everybody else, and yet I am separate from the rest. I am still shaking from head to foot with the excitement I have just experienced, like a bridge over which an ancient iron train has just thundered. I am aware of myself. But only the eye with grit in it, the swelling finger and the bad tooth make themselves felt and are aware of their own individuality. The healthy eye, finger and tooth seem not to exist at all! Surely it is obvious that self-consciousness is merely a disease.

Perhaps I am not a phagocyte any more, efficiently and calmly gobbling up microbes (freckled, and with a pale-blue temple): perhaps I am a microbe and perhaps there are already a thousand amongst us, pretending, like me, to be phagocytes...

What if today's really unimportant incident—what if this is only the beginning, only the first meteorite from a whole series of thundering, burning stones showered by infinity on to our glass paradise?

Summary:

FLOWERS. THE DISSOLVING
OF THE CRYSTAL. IF ONLY.

They say there are flowers that blossom only
once in a hundred years. Why shouldn't there be
flowers that blossom only once in a thousand or
ten thousand years? Perhaps we haven't yet found
out about this because that once-in-a-thousand-
years only came round today.

There am I, blissfully and drunkenly going
downstairs to the duty officer, and quickly, before
my eyes, thousand-year-old buds are bursting
soundlessly before my eyes and there is a blossoming of armchairs, shoes, golden plaques, electric
lamp bulbs, someone's dark, shaggy eyes, the faceted pillars of the banisters, a handkerchief
dropped on the steps, the duty officer's table and,
over it, U's rosy-brown, freckled cheeks. Everything is unusual, new, tender, rosy-red and moist.

U takes the rose ticket from me, and above her
head, through the glass of the wall, the pale-blue,
fragrant moon hangs from an invisible bough. I
point to it triumphantly and say:

"The moon, you understand?"

U looks first at me, then at the ticket number,
and I see that familiar and so charmingly chaste
movement of hers: she straightens the folds of the
unifa between her knees.

"You, my friend, have an abnormal, sickly

141

look, because abnormality and sickness are the same thing. You are destroying yourself, and no one will tell you so, no one."

That "no one" is, of course, equal to the number on the ticket: I-330. Dear, wonderful U! You are right, of course: I am unreasonable, I am sick, I have a soul, I am a microbe. But is not flowering a sickness? Does it not hurt when a bud breaks? And don't you think that the spermatazoon is the most terrifying of all microbes?

I am upstairs in my room. I-330 is sitting in the wide-open cup of the armchair. I am on the floor, embracing her legs, with my head on her knees, and we are silent. Silence, throbbing pulse... I am a crystal, I am dissolving in her, in I-330. I can very distinctly feel how the polished facets that limit me in space are melting, melting away: I am disappearing, I am dissolving in her knees, in all of her, I am becoming less and less, and at the same time ever wider, ever bigger, ever more un-encompassable. Because she is not she, but the Universe. And for a moment I and this joy-permeated armchair near the bed are one: and the magnificently smiling old woman at the door of the Ancient House, and the wild forest behind the Green Wall, and silver ruins against a black background, dreaming like the old woman, and somewhere incredibly far away a door that has just slammed—all this is within me, is with me, is listening to the throbbing of the pulse and is borne through the blissful moment...

In clumsy, confused, submerged words I try to tell her that I am a crystal, and that is why the door is in me, and that is why I feel how happy the armchair is. But I come out with such nonsense that I stop and I feel simply ashamed: I—and suddenly...

"Dearest, forgive me! I just don't understand: I'm talking such nonsense..."

"Why d'you think that talking nonsense is not good? If they cherished and educated human nonsense over the centuries as they do the mind, perhaps something unusually valuable would come of it."

"Yes..." (It seems to me that she's right. How could she not be right at this moment?)

"And just for your nonsense, for what you did yesterday during the promenade, I love you even more than ever."

"Then why did you torture me, why didn't you come, why did you send me your tickets, why did you make me..."

"Supposing I needed to put you to the test? Supposing I needed to know that you would do everything I want—that you are now mine and mine alone?"

"I am—yours and yours alone!"

She took my face, the whole of me, in the palms of her hands and raised my head.

"Well, and how about your obligations of each honourable number?"

Sweet, sharp white teeth; a smile. She is in the open cup of the armchair like a bee: there is a sting in her, and there is honey.

143

Yes, obligations... I mentally leaf through my latest diary notes. And, indeed, nowhere is there even the thought that in essence I ought to...

I say nothing. Rapturously (and perhaps foolishly), I look into the pupils of her eyes, I skip from one to the other and in each of them I see myself: I, tiny, millimetre-sized, am imprisoned in those tiny iridescent cells. And then again bees, lips, the sweet pain of flowering...

In each of us numbers there is a kind of invisible, softly ticking metronome and, without looking at the clock, we can tell the time to within about five minutes. But this time the metronome in me had stopped, I didn't know how much time had passed, and I was so frightened that I snatched my plaque with its watch from under the pillow...

Glory to the Benefactor! Twenty minutes to go! But minutes, when short and docked so absurdly, simply fly past, and I have so much to tell her—everything, my whole self: about O's letter, and about the dreadful evening when I gave her a child; and for some reason about my childhood years, about Plyapa the mathematician, about $\sqrt{-1}$ and how I was at the Unanimity Festival for the first time and wept bitterly, because I had an inkstain on my unifa—a blot of ink on that day of all days.

She raised her head and leaned on her elbow. The two long sharp lines at the corners of her mouth and the dark angle of the upraised brows formed a cross.

"Perhaps on this day..." She stopped and her brows darkened even more. She took my hand and squeezed it tight. "Tell me, you won't forget me, will you? You'll always remember me, won't you?"

"Why do you ask such things? What do you mean, my dear?"

She was silent, and her eyes were already looking past me, through me, they were far away. I suddenly heard the wind buffeting the glass with enormous wings (of course, it had been doing this all the time, but I had only just noticed it), and for some reason I remembered the piercing cries of the birds over the top of the Green Wall.

She tossed her head and shook something off. Once again, for a second, the whole of her touched me, as an aero momentarily bounces off the ground before landing.

"Give me my stockings! Hurry up!"

The stockings had been thrown on to the table, on to the open (193rd) page of my diary. I caught the MS in my haste, the pages scattered and there was no chance of putting them back in order again. Above all, even if I put them together again, it would make no difference, there would be no real order, there would still be rapids, pits, x's.

"I can't bear it," I said. "You're here, beside me, but it's as if you were behind a solid ancient wall. I can hear rustling and voices through the wall, and I can't make out the words, I don't know what's there. I can't bear it. You leave something left unsaid all the time, you haven't even once told me where I got to, over there in the Ancient House, and what corridors those were, and why the doctor—or perhaps it never happened in the first place?"

She rested her hands on my shoulders and slowly, deeply entered into my eyes.

"You want to know everything?"

"Yes, I do. I must."

"And you're not afraid to follow me everywhere, to the end—wherever I might take you?"

"I'll follow you everywhere!"

"Good. I promise you that when the Festival is over, if only... Oh yes, how's your *Integral*? I keep forgetting to ask. Will it be ready soon?"

"No, what did you mean by 'if only'? What were you going to say?"

She (already at the door):

"You'll see for yourself..."

I am alone. All that is left of her is a faintly discernible perfume like the sweet, dry, yellow dust of certain flowers behind the Wall. And something else: some questions that have got their hooks into me, like the ones the ancients used for catching fish (Prehistory Museum).

...Why did she suddenly bring up *Integral*?

Entry No. 24
Summary:

THE LIMIT OF THE FUNCTION. EASTER. DELETE EVERYTHING.

I am like a car being run at excessively high revs; the bearings are red-hot, another moment and molten metal will start dripping and everything will be reduced to nothing. Urgently needed—the cold water of logic. I pour it out in bucketfuls, but the logic sizzles on the hot bearings and evaporates in the air as elusive white steam.

Well, yes, it's clear: to determine the true meaning of the function, you must take its limit. And it's clear that yesterday's foolish "dissolution in the Universe", taken to the limit, is death. Because death is the fullest dissolution of me in the Universe. Hence, if by "L" we denote love and by "D" death, then L=f(D), that is, love and death...

Yes, precisely, precisely. It is because I fear I-330 that I struggle with her. I don't want her. But why are "I don't want" and "I want" side by side in me? This is the horror of it: I want that blissful death of yesterday again. This is the horror of it, that even now, when the logical function has been integrated, when it is obvious that it implicitly contains death within itself, I still want her with my lips, with my arms, with my breast, with every millimetre...

Tomorrow is Unanimity Day. She will be there too, of course, I shall see her, but only from afar. And it will be painful from afar, because I need her, I am irresistibly drawn to be with her, so that her hands, her shoulder, her hair... But I want even that pain. So be it.

Great Benefactor! What an absurdity, to want pain. Everyone understands that pain is negative and that, when added, it reduces the total that we call happiness. Consequently...

And now—no consequently's. Clean. Bare.

A windy, feverishly rosy and disturbing sunset is shining through the glass walls of the house. I turn the armchair round so that that rosiness should not be so obtrusive and I leaf through my diary. And once again I can see how I have forgotten that I'm writing not for myself, but for you, the unknowns whom I love and pity and who are still trailing along somewhere far behind in the remote centuries.

Now, about Unanimity Day, that great day. I have loved it ever since childhood. It seems to me that to us it is something like what their "Easter" was to the ancients. I remember, on the eve of it, I would draw up a calendar of the hours. I would solemnly strike out an hour at a time: one hour lower meant one hour less to wait... If I were sure that no one could see me, I swear on my word of honour that I'd be carrying a calendar like that with me everywhere and would be consulting it to see how much time was left till tomorrow, when I would see, even if only from afar...

(I've been interrupted: they've brought me a new unifa fresh from the workshop. The custom is to issue us with new unifas for Unanimity Day. Footsteps, joyful cries and noise in the corridor.)

But to continue. Tomorrow I shall see the same exciting sight that recurs year after year and stirs the heart in a new way each time: the mighty Cup of Concord, reverently uplifted arms. Tomorrow is the Benefactor's annual election day. Tomorrow we shall again present Him with the keys to the impregnable stronghold of our happiness.

Needless to say, this is not like the chaotic, disorganised elections of the ancients, when, it is amusing to say, even the result of the polls was unknown beforehand. To build a state blindfold, on entirely unconsidered chances,—what could be more senseless? And yet it took centuries for this to be understood.

Need it be said that with us and here, as in everything, there is absolutely no leeway whatever for chance and there can be no surprises. The elections themselves have a meaning that is primarily symbolic: to remind us that we are a single, mighty, million-celled organism; that we are, to quote the "Gospel" of the ancients, the unified Church. Because, throughout the history of the Unified State, there has never been a single case of even one voice daring to violate the majestic chorus in unison.

They say that the ancients carried out their elections secretly, in hiding, like thieves. Some of our historians even assert that voters turned up for the elections celebrations carefully disguised (I can imagine that fantastically grim spectacle: night, the square, figures in dark cloaks stealing along the walls; the purple torch-flames bending over in the wind...). The necessity for all this mystery has never yet been finally explained. The most probable reason is that the elections were associated with mystic, superstitious, perhaps even criminal rites. We, however, have nothing to hide or be ashamed of. We celebrate the elections openly, honourably, in the daytime. I can see all voting for the Benefactor and all can see me voting for Him. Can it be otherwise, when "all" and "I" are a single "We"? How much more ennobling, sincere and lofty this is than the cowardly, underhand "secrecy" of the ancients. And how much more expedient. After all, even if we even assume the impossible, that is, any dissonance in the customary monophony, then the invisible Guardians are here in our ranks. They can immediately identify the numbers that have erred and save them from further false steps and the Unified State from the numbers themselves. And, finally, one more thing...

I can see it through the wall on the left: a woman is hurriedly unbuttoning her unifa in front of the mirror-door of a wardrobe. For a second, vaguely: eyes, lips, two pointed, rosy buds. Then the blinds fall, and in a flash all of yesterday is in me, and I don't know what that "one more thing" is, and I don't want anything to do with it at all! I want one thing: I-330. I want her to be with me every minute, each minute, always, and with me alone. As for what I have just been writing about Unanimity, it's all unnecessary, it's wrong, I want to strike it all out, tear it up and throw it away. Because I know (let it be sacrilege, but it's the truth) that it can be a festival only with her, only if she is beside me, shoulder to shoulder. Without her, tomorrow's sun will be nothing but a tin disc and the sky will be tin painted blue, and I shall be alone.

I snatch up the telephone.

"Is that you?" I say.

"Yes, it is. How late you are!"

"Perhaps it isn't too late yet. I want to ask you... I want you to be with me tomorrow. Darling..."

I say the word 'darling' very softly. And for some reason there is a glimmer of what happened this morning at the shipyard they put a watch under the hundred-ton hammer as a joke: a downstroke, wind in the face, and a hundred-ton, gentle, soft contact with the fragile timepiece.

A pause. I think I can hear someone whispering in her room. Then her voice:

"No, I can't. You understand, if it was up to me... No, I can't. Why? You'll see tomorrow."

Night.

Entry No. 25
Summary:

THE DESCENT FROM HEAVEN.
THE GREATEST CATASTROPHE
IN HISTORY.
THE KNOWN IS OVER.

When, before the beginning, all rose to their feet and the national anthem began swaying over their heads like a slow, ceremonial palanquin—hundreds of Music Factory trumpets and millions of human voices—I forgot everything for a moment: I forgot that disturbing remark of hers about today's festival; I seemed to have forgotten about her altogether. Once again, I was the little boy who had wept on this day because of a tiny stain on his unifa of which only he was aware. Even if no one around could see that I was covered in unwashable black stains, at least I knew that there was no place for me, a criminal, amongst those wide-open faces. Oh, if I could only stand up right now and, choking, shout out everything about myself. Let the end come after that—let it! But if I could only, for just one second, feel as pure and meaningless as that blue sky in all its childlike innocence.

All eyes were turned upwards: in the morning sky, unsullied, still moist with the tears of the nocturnal blue, there was a scarcely discernible spot, now dark, now clad in rays of light. It was He, coming down from the heavens to us, the new Jehovah in an aero, as wise and lovingly cruel as the Jehovah of the ancients. With each passing minute, He came ever closer, and millions of hearts rose still higher towards Him—and now He could see us. And I was mentally surveying the scene from above with Him. The tribune's concentric rings were marked by a pale-blue dotted line like the rings of a spider's web sprinkled with microscopic suns (the glittering of plaques). And now in the centre of it would sit the white, wise Spider, the Benefactor in white robes, sagely binding us hand and foot with the beneficial tenets of happiness.

But now His majestic descent from the heavens was over, the brass of the anthem was silent, all sat down, and I immediately understood that everything is truly a fine spider's web; it is stretched tight, it quivers, at any moment it will snap and something incredible will happen...

Half-rising, I looked round and my glance met lovingly alarmed eyes that were flitting from face to face. Now one raised his hand, scarce moving his fingers, and signalled to another. An answering signal with the finger. And another... I understood: they were Guardians. I understood: they were worried about something, the cobweb was stretched tight, it was trembling. And in me, as in a radio receiver tuned to the same wave-length, there was an answering tremor.

The poet was reciting the pre-election ode on the stage, but I could not hear a single word, only the rhythmic swinging of the hexameter pendulum, and with each swing some kind of appointed hour drew nearer. And I was still feverishly turning over one face after another in the ranks as if they were pages, and still I could not see the one I was looking for, but I must find it as quickly as possible, for the pendulum would tick in a moment, and then— —

He, he, of course. Below, past the stage, gliding over the shining glass travelled the rosy ear-wings, and the speeding body in the form of a letter S was reflected as a double-bent loop: he was trying to get somewhere into the crowded gang-ways between the tribunes.

S and I-330—there was some kind of thread (between them-for me there was always some kind of thread; I didn't yet know what kind, but I would untangle it one of these days). I fixed my eyes on him, he rolled on still further like a ball, with the thread behind him. Now he had stopped, and now...

It was like a high-voltage lightning flash: I was pierced and twisted into a knot. In our rank, about 40 degrees in all away from me, S stopped and bent over. I saw I-330, and with her the re-voltingly negro-lipped, smirking R-13.

My first thought was to rush over there and shout to her, "Why are you with him today? Why didn't you want me?" But the invisible, beneficent spider's web firmly bound my arms and legs. I clenched my teeth and sat like iron, without low-ering my eyes. I remember, as if it were now: that sharp, physical pain in the heart; I remember thinking, "If there can be non-physical causes of physical pain, then it is clear that— —"

Unfortunately, I never arrived at the conclu-sion. I remember a fleeting notion of "soul", and a meaningless ancient saying ran through my head, "one's heart in one's boots". I froze: the hexame-ters stopped. Now it was going to begin... But what?

The five-minute pre-election intermission estab-lished by custom. The pre-election silence estab-lished by custom. But this time it was not as truly prayerful and reverent as always; this time it was as with the ancients when they did not yet know our accumulator towers and when the untamed sky was still occasionally rent by "thunderstorms". This time it was as with the ancients before a storm.

The air was of translucent cast iron. You wanted to breathe, to open your mouth wide. The hearing, strained until it hurt, registered an alarming whisper somewhere behind, like the gnawing of a mouse. With still downcast eyes I could see those two all the time, I-330 and R-13 side by side, shoulder to shoulder, and my hairy hands, so alien, so hateful to me, were trembling on my knees.

All were holding plaques with watches in their hands. One. Two. Three... Five minutes... From the stage came a slow, cast-iron voice:

"Those of you in favour, raise your hands."

If I could only have looked Him in the eyes, as before, directly and devotedly: "Here is all of me. All. Take me!" But this time I did not dare. With an effort, as if all my sinews had gone rusty, I raised my hand.

The rustling of millions of hands. Someone's suppressed "Ah!" And I felt that something had already begun, had been falling headlong, but I did not understand what it was, and I hadn't the strength, I dared not look.

"Who is against?"

This had always been the most solemn moment of the festival: all continued to sit motionless, joyously bowing their heads under the beneficial yoke of the Number of Numbers. But this time I was horrified to hear a rustling sound: as light as a sight, it was more audible than the brass trumpets of the anthem earlier on. Just as a man sighs almost inaudibly for the last time in his life, and all faces around turn pale, all brows are bedewed with cold drops of sweat.

I raised my eyes and—

It took a split second. I saw thousands of hands shoot up—"Against"—and sink down again. I saw I-330's pale face, struck out by a cross, and her raised hand. Everything went dark in front of my eyes.

Another split second, a pause, silence, throbbing pulse. Then, on all tribunes, as if at the sign of a mad conductor, there was a crack, shouts, a flurry of unifas fluttering in flight, the figures of Guardians frantically rushing to and fro, someone's heels in the air right before my eyes and, near the heels, someone's mouth, wide open, straining in an inaudible scream. For some reason, that was what made the most agonising impression of all: thousands of silently shrieking mouths, as on a monstrously enormous screen.

And, as on a screen, somewhere far below me for a second, O's white lips; pressed back against a wall in a passage, she was standing and shielding her stomach with her crossed arms. And suddenly she was gone, swept away, or I forgot about her, because...

It was not on a screen this time, it was in me,

in my constricted heart, in my rapidly throbbing temples. Over my head, to the left, on a bench, R-13 suddenly jumped out—spluttering, red-faced, frantic. He was carrying I-330 in his arms. She was pale, her unifa was torn open from the shoulder to the breast and there was blood on the white. She was holding firmly on to his neck, and in enormous bounds, from bench to bench, as revoltingly agile as a gorilla, he was carrying her upwards.

It was a fire in the time of the ancients—everything turned red and there was only one thing to do: jump up and overtake them. I cannot now explain to myself where I found the strength, but I went through the crowd like a battering ram, leapt on to someone's shoulders, then on to the benches until I was close enough to grip him by the collar.

"Don't you dare! Don't you dare, I said! Let her go at once!" (Fortunately, my voice was inaudible: all were shouting their own words, all were fleeing.)

"Who are you? What is it? What's the matter?" He looked round and his spluttering lips trembled. He probably thought he had been apprehended by one of the Guardians.

"I won't have it, I won't allow it, that's what's the matter! Put her down! At once!"

But he only smacked his lips furiously, ducked his head and ran on further. And at this point—I'm unbelievably ashamed to be writing this, but I think I should do so nevertheless; I should write it down so that you, my unknown readers, may study the history of my illness to the full—at this point I swung my arm back and hit him on the head. You see? I hit him! I remember it distinctly. And I also remember a feeling of liberation, of relief all through my body because of that blow.

She quickly slipped down from his grasp.

"Go away!" she shouted at R. "You can see he's... Go away, R, go away!"

R bared his white, negroid teeth, spluttered a word in my face, dived down and disappeared. I picked her up, held her close to me and carried her away.

My heart was thudding; it was enormous, and with each beat it sent out such a turbulent, stormy, hot wave of joy. What did it matter if something had flown to pieces, had been smashed to smithereens back there! Just so long as I was carrying, carrying, carrying her...

Evening, 22 hours.

It's an effort for me to hold the pen in my hand: such immeasurable exhaustion after all the vertiginous events of the morning. Have the protective, centuries-old walls of the Unified State really collapsed? Are we really without a roof again and in a wild state of freedom, like our remote ancestors? Is there really no Benefactor? Against... on Unanimity Day—against? I am ashamed, hurt, terrified for them. And incidentally, who are "they"? And who am I: "they" or "we"? Do I really know?

There she is, sitting on the sun-warmed glass bench to which I carried her, on the very highest tribune. Her right shoulder is uncovered and so, lower down, is the beginning of a wonderful and incalculable curve; a thin red snake of blood. She seems not to notice that it is blood, that her breast is bare... No, there is more to it than that: she can see all this, but it is what she needs now, and if her unifa was buttoned up, she would tear it open, she would...

"But tomorrow..." She breathes eagerly through clenched, gleaming sharp teeth. "But tomorrow there's no knowing what will happen. You must understand, I don't know, and no one else knows either—it's just not known! D'you understand that everything that was known is over. Now it's the new, the incredible, the unseen."

Down below, they're foaming at the mouth, rushing about, screaming. But that's far away and receding too, because she is looking at me, she is slowly drawing me into herself through the narrow gold windows in the pupils of her eyes. She continues like that for a long time without speaking. And for some reason I remember how once, through the Green Wall, I also looked into a pair of unfathomable yellow eyes, and birds were wheeling over the Wall (or that was at some other time).

"Listen, if nothing unusual happens tomorrow, I'll take you there. You understand?"

No, I don't understand. But I nod silently. I have dissolved, I am infinitely small, I am a point... After all, this condition of being a point has its own logic (today's): there are more unknowns in a point than in anything else: it only has to move or stir, and it can turn into thousands of different curves or hundreds of bodies.

I'm terrified to move: what shall I turn into? And it seems to me that all the rest, like myself, are afraid to make the slightest movement. Now, as I write this, they are all sitting secluded in their glass cells and are waiting for something. No buzzing of the lift, usual at this time, no laughter, no footsteps. Sometimes I see two together, looking over their shoulders, tiptoeing along the corridor, whispering...

What's going to happen tomorrow? What shall I turn into tomorrow?

Entry No. 26
Summary:

THE WORLD EXISTS. THE RASH. 41°.

Morning. The sky through the ceiling is, as always, strong, round, red-cheeked. I think I would be less surprised if I saw overhead an unusual four-cornered sun, people in multicoloured clothes of animal skins, and impenetrable stone walls. So does our world perhaps still exist? Or is it only inertia: the generator has already been switched

160

off, but the gearwheels are still rumbling and spinning—two revolutions, three revolutions, but stopping during the fourth...

Are you familiar with this strange condition? At night you wake up, open your eyes in the dark and suddenly feel that you've lost your way, and quickly, quickly you begin to feel round you, to try and find something familiar and solid—a wall, a lamp, a chair. That was how I fumbled round me, looking in the Unified State Newspaper: quick, quick—ah, here it is.

"Unanimity Day, long and impatiently awaited by all, finally took place yesterday. For the 48th time, the same Benefactor was unanimously elected who has demonstrated his unshakeable wisdom so many times. The ceremony was darkened by a certain confusion caused by the enemies of happiness, who thereby, naturally, deprived themselves of the right to be the bricks of the Unified State's foundation, renewed yesterday. It is clear to each and every one that to take account of their votes would be as stupid as to take the coughing of sick people fortuitously present in a concert hall for a magnificent, heroic symphony..."

O wise one! Are we really all saved, in spite of everything? But what answer can possibly be made to that most crystalline syllogism?

Further on, another two lines:

"Today, a combined session of the Administrative Bureau, the Medical Bureau and the Guardians' Bureau is to be held at 12. An important State Act is about to be passed."

11 – 1578

No, the walls were still standing—there they were, I could feel them. And gone was the terrifying sensation that I was lost, that I was goodness knows where, that I had gone astray; and it wasn't in the least surprising that I could see a blue sky and a round sun; and everybody was leaving for work as usual.

I walked along the prospekt with particular firmness, my footsteps ringing, and it seemed to me that all were walking like me. Then came a crossing, a turn round the corner, and I could see that everybody was avoiding the corner of the building in a strange sort of way; it was as if a pipe had burst in the wall and was squirting out cold water, so that it was impossible to walk along the pavement.

Another five, then ten paces, and I too was doused with cold water, rocked, forced off the pavement... On the wall, at a height of approximately two metres, there was a rectangular sheet of paper flaunting the incomprehensible, poisonously green letters:

MEPHISTO

Below—an eloquently bowed back and ear-wings that were transparently quivering with rage or agitation. Raising his right hand and helplessly pulling back the left, like a wounded wing, he was jumping up to tear off the paper, but he couldn't make it, he was just too short.

Every passer-by probably had the same thought:

"If I go up, the only one of all these people, won't he think I'm in some way to blame, which is precisely why I want..."

I admit that the same thought occurred to me. But I remembered how many times he had been my true guardian-angel and how many times he had rescued me, so I boldly approached him, reached up and tore down the sheet of paper.

S turned round, quickly drilled me to the bottom and extracted something from there. Then he raised his left eyebrow and winked at the wall, on which hung "Mephisto". And I glimpsed the tail-end of his smile which, to my surprise, was even merry. But then what was there to be surprised about? To the exhausting, slowly rising temperature of the incubation period, a doctor will always prefer a rash and a forty-degree fever: at least in this case the nature of the illness is clear. "Mephisto", which was being posted up on the walls that day, was the rash. I could understand his smile...[1]

The descent into the underground, and on the spotless glass of the steps, another white sheet of paper: "Mephisto". And more—on the wall below, on a bench, on a mirror in the carriage (evidently posted up in haste—it was lopsided and twisted)—everywhere the same eerie white rash.

In the silence, the distinct buzzing of the wheels was like the noise of inflamed blood. Someone was

[1] I must admit that I did not find the exact explanation for this smile until after many days crammed with the most strange and unexpected events.

touched on the shoulder: he shuddered and dropped his roll of papers. On my left was another, reading the same line in the newspaper, the same line, the same line, and the newspaper was trembling almost imperceptibly. I could feel that everywhere, in wheels, in arms, in newspapers, in eyelashes, the pulse was beating faster and faster and perhaps today, when I and I-330 got there, the temperature would be 39, 40, 41 degrees, marked with a black line on the thermometer...

At the shipyard there was the same silence, buzzing like a faraway, invisible propeller. The lathes stood there, scowling mutely. Only the cranes almost inaudibly, as if on tiptoe, were gliding to and fro, bending over, picking up pale-blue lumps of frozen air in their claws and loading them into the on-board cisterns of *Integral*. We were already preparing her for the test flight.

"Well, will we finish loading in a week?"

I was speaking to the Second Constructor. His face was porcelain, decorated with sweetly pale-blue, tenderly pink flowers (eyes, lips), but today they seemed wilted and blurred. We were estimating aloud, but I suddenly stopped in mid-word and stood there gaping: high under the dome on a pale-blue lump hoisted up by a crane was a scarcely discernible white square—a piece of paper stuck on to it. I began shaking all over, perhaps with laughter. Yes, I could hear myself laughing (d'you know what it's like to hear your own laughter?).

"No, listen," I said. "Imagine you're on an ancient aeroplane, the altimeter reads five thousand metres, the wing has come off, you've gone into a spin and on the way down you're calculating, 'Tomorrow, from twelve to two ... from two to six ... dinner at six...' Ridiculous, isn't it? But that's exactly what we're doing now!" The little blue flowers stirred and goggled. What if I were of glass and could not see that in some three to four hours' time?..

Entry No. 27

Summary:

NO SUMMARY—IT'S FORBIDDEN.

I am alone in endless corridors, the same ones. A blank concrete wall. Somewhere, water is dripping on to stone. The familiar, heavy, opaque door, and a dull roar from the other side.

She had said she would come out to me at 16 precisely. But it's already five past 16, ten past, fifteen past, and still nobody has appeared.

For a second I am the former I, who will be terrified if that door opens. Five more minutes, and if she doesn't come out— —

Somewhere, water is dripping on to stone. No one. I feel with yearning joy that I have been saved. I go slowly back along the corridor. The trembling dotted line of little lamp bulbs on the ceiling grows dimmer and dimmer...

Suddenly, the hasty clang of a door behind me, a quick tapping that rebounds softly off the ceiling and the walls, and she, flying, slightly out of breath with running, breathes with her mouth:

"I knew you'd be here, I knew you'd come! I knew: you, you..."

The lances of her eyelashes move up to admit me... How can I describe what it does to me, that ancient, stupid, marvellous rite when her lips touch mine? What formula can I use to express this whirlwind that blows away everything in my soul except her? Yes, yes, in my soul—go on, laugh, if you want to.

With an effort she slowly opens her eyelids and with an effort slowly utters the words:

"No, enough... Later. Now—let's go."

The door opens. Steps, old and worn. And an intolerably confused din, whistling, light...

*　*　*

Almost twenty-four hours have passed since then, everything in me has subsided slightly, and yet it is still extremely difficult for me to give even an approximately accurate description. It's as if a bomb had been exploded in my head, and open mouths, wings, shouts, leaves, words, stones—close to me, in a heap, one after another...

I remember that my first thought had been, "Quick, back as fast as you can." Because it was clear to me: while I was waiting there in the corridors, they had somehow blown up or destroyed the Green Wall, and everything had rushed in from behind there and had swamped our city that had been purged of the lower world.

I must have said something of the sort to her. She laughed.

"Not at all! We've simply come out on the other side of the Green Wall..." Then I opened my eyes, and face to face with me, in real life was something that, until then, no living person had ever seen otherwise than reduced a thousand times, weakened, dimmed by the turbid glass of the Wall.

The sun... It was not our sun, evenly distributed over the mirror surface of the roadways: it was living fragments, ceaselessly jumping spots which dazzled the eyes and made the head spin. And the trees were like candles pointing up into the sky; like spiders squatting close to the ground on crooked legs; like mute green fountains... And all this was squatting, stirring, rustling, some kind of bristly little ball scuttled out from under my feet, and I was riveted to the spot, I couldn't move a step, because it wasn't a flat surface underfoot, you understand, it wasn't a flat surface, but something revoltingly soft, yielding, alive, green and springy.

I was deafened by all this and I choked—this is perhaps the most suitable word. I stood, clutching a waving bough with both hands.

"It's all right, it's all right! That's only the beginning, it'll pass off! Be brave!" Next to I-330, on the green, vertiginously dancing gauze, I saw someone's profile, as thin as if cut out of paper... No, not someone's. I knew the man. I remembered him, it was the doctor—no, no, I understood everything very clearly. And I also understood that both had gripped me under the arms and were laughing as they pulled me forward. I kept stumbling and slipping. There was croaking over there, moss, mounds, cackling, branches, tree-trunks, wings, leaves, whistling...

Then the trees parted, and there was a bright glade, and there were people in the glade... But I don't really know: perhaps it would be more accurate to call them creatures.

This was the most difficult part. Because this exceeded all the bounds of credibility. And it is now clear to me why she had always kept so stubbornly silent: I wouldn't have believed, even her. It may be that tomorrow I shan't even believe myself and this entry I am making.

On the glade, around a bare, skull-like rock, there was a noisy crowd of three or four hundred ... people. Let them be people, I find it hard to put it otherwise. Just as one spots only the familiar faces among the general mass on the tribunes, so did I only see our grey-blue unifas at first. Then, a second later, and among the unifas, they stood out quite distinctly and simply: raven-black, ginger, gold, dark bay, roan and white people—they looked like human beings. All were unclothed and all were covered with a short, glossy wool like the kind anyone can see on the dummy horse in the Prehistoric Museum. But the females had the same faces, yes, exactly the same faces as our own women: delicately rosy and not covered with hair; their breasts were also free of hair—big, firm, of beautiful geometric form. The males had only part of their faces uncovered by hair, like our ancestors.

It was so incredible, so unexpected, that I stood calmly there—I positively insist on this—I stood calmly there and just stared. As with scales: overload one pan and then you can put as much on the other as you like, but the pointer still won't move.

Suddenly, I was alone: she wasn't with me any more, and I didn't know how she had disappeared or where to. Around me were only those people, their fur shining silkily in the sun. I clutched at someone's hot, firm, raven-black shoulder.

"Listen, for the Benefactor's sake, you didn't see where she went, did you? Just now, just this moment..."

Shaggy, stern brows turned on me.

"Sh-sh-sh! Quiet!" And they nodded shaggily towards the middle, to the rock as yellow as a skull.

I saw her there, on the summit, above the heads of the crowd. The sun was shining from over there straight into my eyes, so that, against the dark-blue band of the sky, she was sharply defined, charcoal-black, a charcoal silhouette on blue. Some clouds were flying past a little higher up; they looked like rocks, not clouds, and she herself on a rock, and behind her the crowd, and the glade were soundlessly gliding along like a ship, and the light Earth was floating away underfoot.

"Brothers!..." It was her speaking. "Brothers! You all know they're building *Integral* out there on the other side of the Wall, in the city. And you know that the day has come when we shall destroy that Wall—all walls—so that the green wind may blow from one end of the Earth to the other. But *Integral* will carry those walls younder, up there, into thousands of other worlds that will make their lights twinkle for you through the dark nocturnal leaves tonight..."

Waves, foam, wind beating on the rock.

"Down with *Integral!* Down with it!"

"No, brothers, not down with it. For *Integral* must be ours. On the day when it first casts off into the sky, we shall be on board. Because the Constructor of *Integral* is with us. He has left the walls, he has come here with me to be amongst you. Long live the Constructor!"

In no time at all I am somewhere up on high and under me are heads, heads, heads, wide-shouting mouths, arms flung up and falling again. It was uncommonly strange and intoxicating: I felt that I was above all the rest, I was I, a separate entity, a world, I had ceased to be an addendum, as always, and had become a unit.

And then I was down below, near the rock, with my body squashed, happy and crumpled, as after amorous embraces. The sun, voices from above—her smile. A woman, golden-haired with a satin golden skin and fragrant with herbs. She was holding a goblet, apparently of wood. She sipped from it with red lips and handed it to me and, thirstily, with my eyes closed, I drank to quench the fire, I drank sweet, cold and prickly sparks.

And then the blood in me, like the whole world, was racing a thousand times faster, the light Earth was flying like thistle-down. And to me everything was easy, and simple, and clear.

Then I saw on the rock the familiar, enormous letters, "Mephisto", and for some reason this had to be, it was the simple, firm thread binding everything together. I could see a crude picture—perhaps on that rock: a winged youth with a transparent body, and where his heart ought to have been there was a blinding, raspberry-red, glowing coal. And again I understood that coal... no, that is wrong, I could feel it, just as, without hearing them, I could feel every word (she was talking from above, from the rock), and I felt that all were breathing together, and all had somewhere to fly to together, as the birds did that time over the Wall...

From behind, from the heavily breathing thicket of bodies, a loud voice:

"But this is madness!"

Apparently it was I, yes, I think it was I and none other who bounded up on to the rock, and from there the sun, heads, a green serrated saw against the blue, and I shouted:

"Yes, yes, exactly! And all of us must go mad, as soon as possible. It's essential, that much I know."

She is beside me; her smile is two dark lines running upwards at an angle from the corners of her mouth; and there is a coal of fire in me, and this is momentary, light, almost painful, beautiful...

And then—nothing but stuck, disjointed fragments.

Slowly, flying low—a bird. I can see it is alive, like me, it is like a human being, it turns its head to the right, to the left, and round black eyes drill into me...

More: a back covered with glassy wool the colour of old ivory. A dark insect with tiny, transparent wings is crawling over it. The back twitches to drive off the insect, and twitches again...

More: the leaves cast a shade that is woven and latticed. They are lying in the shade and eating something similar to the legendary food of the ancients: a long yellow fruit and a piece of something dark. A woman pushes some into my hand, and I am amused: I don't know if I can eat it.

And again: a crowd, heads, feet, hands, mouths. Faces leap out for a second and disappear, they burst like bubbles. And for a second, or perhaps I only imagine it—transparent, flying wing-ears.

I squeezed her hand with all my might. She looked round.

"What's the matter?"

"He's here... Or so it seemed to me..."

"Who's he?"

"Just now—in the crowd..."

Charcoal-black, thin brows tilted up to the temples: an acute triangle, a smile. It wasn't clear to me why she was smiling. How could she smile?

"You don't understand. You don't understand what it means if he or any other one of them is here."

"You're funny! How could it ever enter anyone's head on that side of the Wall that we're here? Remember, you're here now, but did you ever think it was possible? They catch us over there, so let them. You're drivelling."

She smiled lightly and cheerfully, and I smiled too; intoxicated, merry and light, the Earth was floating through the air...

Entry No. 28
Summary:

BOTH. ENTROPY AND ENERGY.
THE OPAQUE PART OF THE BODY.

Now if your world is like the world of our remote ancestors, then imagine that you once came upon a sixth or seventh part of the world in the ocean, a kind of Atlantis, and there were incredible labyrinth-cities, people sailing through the air without the aid of wings or aeros, rocks levitated by the force of a look—in a word, something that could never enter your head even if you were suffering from hallucinations. Well, that's how it was with me yesterday. Because—please understand me—since the time of the Two Hundred Years War, not one of us has ever been over the Wall, as I have already told you.

I know that it is my duty to you, my unknown friends, to tell you in as much detail as possible about the strange and unexpected world that was revealed to me yesterday. But for the time being I am in no state to return to this subject. An endless succession of surprises, a downpour of events, and it is more than I can do to collect it all: I lift the hem of my unifa, I hold out my cupped hands, but whole bucketsful come down beyond my reach and only a few drops fall on to these pages...

First, I heard loud voices outside my door and recognised I-330's resilient and metallic voice, and another, almost as inflexible as a wooden ruler—U's voice. Then the door burst open with a bang and shot both of them into my room. Just that: shot them in.

I-330 put her hand on the back of my armchair and, over her shoulder, to the right, smiled at the other, but only with her teeth. I would not like to have stood within range of that smile.

"Listen," said I-330 to me, "this woman has apparently set herself the task of protecting you like a little-boy from me. Is this with your permission?"

Then the other woman, her gills quivering:

"But that's what he is, a little boy! Yes! It's only because he can't even see that everything you're up to with him is purely so as to ... that it's all a comedy. Yes. And it is my duty..."

For a fraction of a second I saw the broken, dancing straight line of my eyebrows in the mirror. I leapt to my feet and, restraining with an effort my other self, my hairy fists shaking, forcing each word through my teeth with an effort, I shouted straight at her, straight into the gills:

"Get out—this minute! This minute!"

The gills swelled to a brick-red, then went limp and turned grey. She opened her mouth to speak, then clammed up and went out slamming the door behind her.

I rushed over to I-330.

"I shan't forgive myself, I shan't ever forgive myself for this! She dared to insult you? But you simply mustn't think that I think that... that she... It's all because she wants to get registered to me, but I..."

"Fortunately, she won't be in time to get registered. And even if there were a thousand like her, it makes no difference to me. I know you'll believe not the thousand, but only me. Because after what happened yesterday... I'm all yours, all the way, as you wanted. I'm in your hands, and at any moment you can..."

"At any moment—what?" And I immediately realised what; the blood rushed to my ears and into my cheeks, and I shouted, "You mustn't speak of that, never talk to me about that! After all, that was the other I, you understand, the former I, but now..."

"Who knows? A man is like a novel, there's no telling till the last page how it will end. Otherwise it wouldn't be worth the trouble of reading it..."

She was stroking my head. I couldn't see her face, but I could tell from her voice that she was looking somewhere very far away; her eyes were staring beyond a cloud that was sailing silently and slowly into the unknown...

Suddenly she pushed me firmly but gently away with her hand.

"Listen, I came to tell you that perhaps these are the last few days that we... You know all the auditoriums have been cancelled as from this evening."

"Cancelled?"

"Yes. I was walking past and I noticed it: they're preparing something in the auditorium buildings; there were tables and medics in white."

"What does it mean?"

"I don't know. No one knows yet. And that's the worst of it. I just have an intuition: they've switched on the current, there's a spark running along—and if not now, then tomorrow... But perhaps they won't make it in time."

I had long since given up trying to understand who they were and who we were. I didn't know whether I wanted them to make it in time or not. Only one thing was clear to me: she was walking along the very brink, and any moment now...

"But that's madness," I said. "You versus the Unified State. You might just as well plug the muzzle with your hand and think you can hold back the shot. Sheer madness!"

A smile.

"'And all must go mad, it's essential for all to go mad, and as soon as possible!' Someone said that yesterday. Remember? Over there..."

Yes, I've got it written down. Consequently, it must have really happened. I looked silently at her face: the dark cross on it was particularly vivid at that moment.

"My dear, before it's too late... If you want, I'll drop everything, forget everything, and we'll go together to the other side of the Wall, to those... I don't know who they are."

She shook her head. Through the dark windows of her eyes, there, within her, I could see a stove blazing, sparks, tongues of flame leaping upwards, stacks of dry, resinous firewood piled up ready. And it was clear to me that it was too late, my words could not achieve anything now...

She stood up, ready to leave. Perhaps the last days were at hand, or even the last minutes... I gripped her hand.

"No! Just a little longer, for the sake of... for the sake of..."

She slowly raised my hand up to the light, the hairy hand that I hated so much. I wanted to pull it away, but she held it tight.

"Your hand... After all, you don't know, and not many do, that women from here, from the city, have happened to love those other ones. And there are probably a few drops of sunny forest blood in you. That is probably why it is you that I— —"

A pause, and how strange it is: from the pause, from the emptiness, from nothing, my heart was racing. And I cried out:

"Aha! You won't go yet! You won't go until

177

you tell me about them, because you love ... them, but I don't even know who they are or where they come from. Who are they? The half we lost, H_2 and O; but in order to get H_2—rivulets, streams, waterfalls, waves, storms—the halves have to combine..."

I can distinctly remember her every movement. I remember how she took my glass set-square from the table and, all the time I was talking, she was pressing its sharp edge against her cheek so that a white scar appeared on it, then the white was suffused with pink and the scar disappeared. And, amazingly, I cannot remember her words, especially at the beginning; only certain disconnected images and colours.

I know that it was about the Two Hundred Years War at first. And there was red on the green of the grasses, on the dark clays, on the blue of the snows—red, undrying puddles. Then yellow grasses scorched by the sun, and naked, yellow, dishevelled people, and scraggy dogs close by, near the bloated carrion of dogs, or perhaps of human beings... This, of course, was outside the walls, because the city had already been victorious, the city already had our present-day oil food.

And almost from the sky down to the bottom, black, heavy folds, and the folds are wavering: slow columns, smoke over the forests and over the villages. A muffled howling: endless black lines of people are being herded into the city so that they can be forcibly saved and taught happiness.

"You almost knew all this?"

178

"Yes, almost."

"But you didn't know, and only a few knew, that a small part of them nevertheless survived and stayed outside the Walls to go on living. Naked, they went into the forests. They learned there from the trees, the wild beasts, the birds, the flowers and the sun. They grew fur all over, but underneath the fur they kept their warm red blood. It's worse for you: in the city, you are all overgrown with figures, they crawl over you like lice. You must all be stripped and driven into the forests. Let people learn to tremble with fear, with joy, with insane wrath, with cold, let them pray to fire. And we, the Mephistos, we want..."

"No, wait. About 'Mephisto'. What is 'Mephisto'?"

"Mephisto? It's an ancient name, it's the one who... You remember, over there, on the rock, there was a picture of a youth... But no, I'd do better to talk your language, then you'll be more likely to understand. You see, there are two forces in the world, entropy and energy. The first leads towards blissful peace, to happy equilibrium; the other, to the destruction of equilibrium, to agonisingly perpetual motion. Entropy was worshipped as God by our, or rather by your ancestors. But we anti-Christians, we..."

And then just at that moment—a knock on the door as inaudible as a whisper, and into the room rushed the same squashed one with his forehead jammed down over his eyes, the one who had brought me notes from I-330 a number of times.

179

He hurried up to us, stopped, panting like an air-pump and couldn't utter a word. He must have been running at full pelt.

"Come on, then! What's happened?" She gripped him by the arm

"They're coming—here..." gasped the pump at last. 'The guards... And that, how should I put it, that hunchbacked character is with them."

"S?"

"That's the one! Right close by in the house. They'll be here soon. Hurry, hurry!"

"Never mind! There's no hurry..." She laughed, and there were sparks and merry tongues of fire in her eyes.

This was either stupid, senseless courage, or there was something in it I didn't yet understand.

"For the Benefactor's sake," I exclaimed. 'You've got to understand that this..."

"For the Benefactor's sake,"—the sharp triangle of a smile.

"All right then, for my sake... Please."

"Ah, but there was one more thing that you and I had to... Oh well, never mind. Tomorrow..."

She nodded at me cheerfully (yes, cheerfully) and so did he, emerging for a second from under his forehead awning. And I was alone.

I quickly sat down at the table. I opened my notes, took a pen, so that they would find me working on behalf of the Unified State. Suddenly, every hair on my head was alive, separate and standing up. "What if they read even only one of the last few pages?"

I sat at the table, not moving, and saw the walls shaking, the pen quivering in my hand, the letters wavering and merging...

Hide them? But where, when everything is glass? Burn them? But that would be seen from the corridor and the neighbouring rooms. Besides, I was unable, I hadn't the strength to destroy that agonising and perhaps most precious piece of myself.

Voices and footsteps already, far down the corridor. I only just had time to snatch up the stack of pages and push them under me, and there I was, riveted to the armchair which was quivering in every atom, and the floor underfoot was a ship's deck heaving up and down...

Shrinking into a ball, cowering under the awning of my forehead, I covertly managed to see them from under my eyebrows: they were walking from room to room, starting at the right end of the corridor and working their way steadily nearer. Some of the occupants were sitting motionless, like me, others were dashing out to meet them and were flinging the door wide open, the lucky ones! If only I could have done that too...

"Virtue is a highly perfected form of disinfection essential to humanity, and as a result of this, no peristalsis whatever in the organism of the Unified State..." I was grinding out this utter balderdash and was bending lower and lower over the table, but there was a mad foundryworks in my head; my back heard the doorhandle rattle, there was a puff of wind and my armchair began dancing under me...

Only then did I detach myself from the page with an effort and turn to the newcomers (how hard it is to act out a comedy... Oh, who was talking to me about comedy today?). In front of me was S, gloomily, silently and rapidly, with his eyes, drilling wells in me, in my chair, in the sheets of paper quivering under my hand. Then, for a moment, familiar, everyday faces in the doorway, and one of them detached itself—swelling, rosy-brown gills...

I remembered everything that had happened in this room half an hour previously, and it was clear to me that she was now—— My whole being was throbbing and pulsating in that (fortunately opaque) part of the body which I had covered with the manuscript.

U went up to S from behind, touched him cautiously on the sleeve and said softly:

"This is D-503, the Constructor of *Integral*. You've heard of him, no doubt? He's always at his desk like this... He doesn't spare himself at all!"

...And I thought, "What a marvellous, wonderful woman."

S slithered across to me and bent over my shoulder to look at the desk. I moved my elbow to cover what I had written, but he shouted sternly:

"Kindly show me what you've got there at once!"

Flushed with shame, I handed him the sheet of paper. He read it, and I saw a smile leap out of his eyes, dive down his face and, its tail barely

182

wriggling, come to rest somewhere in the right corner of his mouth.

"Somewhat ambiguous, but still... All right, then, carry on. We shall trouble you no further."

He slapped off to the door like paddles over water, and with each step he took I gradually recovered the use of my legs, arms and fingers. My soul redistributed itself evenly over my whole body and I breathed again...

Finally: U stayed behind in my room, came up to me, bent down and whispered in my ear:

"Luckily for you, I..."

I could not understand. What did she mean?

In the evening, later, I learned that they had taken three people with them. Incidentally, no one is speaking aloud about this, or about anything else that is happening (the educative influence of the Guardians invisibly present in our midst). Conversations are mainly about the rapid fall of the barometer and a change in the weather.

Entry No. 29
Summary:

FILAMENTS ON THE FACE.
SHOOTS.
UNNATURAL COMPRESSION.

Strange: the barometer is falling, but there's still no wind and all's quiet. A storm has already started up there, but we can hardly hear it. The clouds are racing along at full speed. There are still only a few of them—separate, jagged fragments. It's as if a city had been overthrown up above and the debris of walls and towers are plunging downwards, swelling in front of the eyes with terrifying speed as they come nearer and nearer; but they will fly through pale-blue infinity for days before finally crashing down amongst us on to the bottom.

Below, all is quiet. There are fine, baffling, almost invisible filaments in the air. They are borne over every autumn from the other side, from behind the Wall. They float slowly, and suddenly you feel something extraneous and invisible on your face. You want to brush it off, but no, you can't, no matter how hard you try...

There are particularly many of these filaments if you go near the Green Wall, where I was walking this morning. I-330 had made a date with me in the Ancient House, in our special "flat".

I was already going past the hulk of the Ancient House when I heard someone's mincing, hasty footsteps and hurried breathing behind me. I looked round. O was catching me up. The whole of her was somehow, in a special way, totally and resiliently round. Her arms, and the cups of her breasts, and all her body, so familiar to me, were all rounding and stretching her unifa. She looked as though she might burst through the thin fabric at any moment and come out into the sunlight, into the open. I imagined how over there, in the green forest thickets, the shoots burst up through

184

the ground just as stubbornly in spring so as to throw out branches, leaves and blossoms as soon as possible.

She was silent for several seconds, her blue eyes shining straight at me.

"I saw you there, on Unanimity Day."

"I saw you too..." And I suddenly remembered how she had been standing down below in a narrow passage, pressing herself back against the wall and covering her stomach with her hands. I involuntarily looked at her round stomach under the unifa.

She evidently noticed, and became all roundedly rosy and rosy smile.

"I'm so happy, so happy... I'm full, you understand, full to the brim. I walk about and I can't hear what's round me, and I'm listening inwardly all the time, to myself..."

I said nothing. There was something extraneous on my face, it was getting in the way and I just couldn't shake it off. Suddenly, her blue eyes shining even more brightly, she clutched my hand and I felt her lips on it... It was the first time in my life that this had happened to me. It was a kind of hitherto unfamiliar, ancient caress, and it caused me such shame and pain that I (perhaps even roughly) pulled my hand away.

"Listen, you've gone out of your mind! And not so much that as you've completely... What are you feeling so happy about? Can you really have forgotten what you're in for? Not now, but in a month, in two months just the same..."

185

She looked crestfallen: all her curves bent inwards, were deformed. But in my own heart there was the unpleasant and even morbid compression associated with a sensation of pity (the heart is nothing other than the ideal pump; compression, the suction of liquid by a pump, is a technical absurdity; from which it is clear how fundamentally absurd, unnatural and morbid are all the "loves", "pities" and so on that evoke such compression).

Silence. The murky green glass of the Wall on the left. A dark-red mass ahead. And those two colours, combining, gave me what seemed like a brilliant idea in the form of a resultant.

"Stop! I know how to save you. I'll deliver you from seeing your child and then dying. You'll be able to nurse it, you'll watch it growing in your arms, getting chubby, filling out like a fruit..."

She trembled from head to foot and fixed her eyes on me.

"You remember that woman ... well, then, a long time ago, on the promenade. She's here right now, in the Ancient House. Let's go and see her, and I swear I'll get you fixed up without delay."

I could already see myself and I-330 conducting her along the corridors— there she was already, among the flowers, the grasses, the leaves... But she stepped back from me, and the horns of her rosy crescent were trembling and curving downwards.

"She's that very woman," she said.

"Well..." For some reason I felt embarrassed. "Well, yes, that very woman."

"And you want me to go to her, to ask her so that I... Don't ever dare mention that to me again!"

With her shoulders bowed, she walked quickly away from me. As if she had remembered something else, she turned round and called:

"And I shall die, yes. So be it! It's got nothing to do with you—what do you care?"

Silence. Pieces of blue towers and walls are falling from above and growing bigger and bigger with terrifying speed in front of my eyes, but they still have hours, perhaps even days, to fly through infinity. The invisible filaments float slowly and settle on my face, and there is no way of brushing them off, there is no way of removing them.

I walk slowly towards the Ancient House. There is an absurd, excruciating compression in my heart...

Entry No. 30
Summary:
THE LAST NUMBER. GALILEO'S ERROR. IS IT NOT BETTER?

Here is my conversation with I-330 yesterday in the Ancient House, amid the mrtticoloured noise—red, green, bronze-yellow and white—that drowned the logical process of thought... And, aH the time, under the marble smile of the ancient snub-nosed poet.

I am reproducing this conversation word for

187

word because I think it will be of decisive significance for the destiny of the Unified State and more, for the Universe. And besides, you, my unknown readers, will perhaps find some justification for me here...

She dumped it all on me at once, without any preliminaries.

"I know you're having the first test flight of *Integral* the day after tomorrow. That's when we're going to get our hands on it."

"What? The day after tomorrow?"

"Yes. Sit down, don't get into a state. We can't afford to lose a minute. There were twelve Mephistos among the hundreds selected at random by the Guardians yesterday. If we let two or three days go by, they're doomed."

I said nothing.

"To observe the course of the test, electrical engineers, mechanics, doctors and meteorologists will be sent to you. And at twelve precisely, remember this, when the dinner-bell rings and all go into the dining-room,'we shall stay behind in the corridor and lock everybody up in the dining-room—and then *Integral* will be ours... You understand, this move is absolutely vital. *Integral* in our hands will be the weapon which will enable us to finish everything at once, quickly and painlessly. As for their aeros—pooh! They will simply be insignificant mosquitoes against a kite. And then, if it's unavoidable, it will be possible to deflect the engine jets downwards and this alone..."

I jumped to my feet.

"That's unthinkable! It's stupid! Don't you realise what you're plotting? That's revolution!"

"Yes, revolution! Why is it stupid?"

"It's stupid because there cannot be a revolution. Because our—this is not you talking, this is me—our revolution was the last one. There cannot be any more revolutions. Everyone knows that..."

A mocking, sharp triangle of eyebrows:

"My dear, you're a mathematician. Even more, you're a philosopher of mathematics. So tell me the last number."

"Meaning what? I ... I don't understand. What last number?"

"Why, the last, the highest, the biggest."

"But that's stupid. Since the number of numbers is infinite, how can you want a last one?"

"Then what last revolution do you want? There's no last one, revolutions are infinite. The last one is for children: children are frightened of infinity, and it's essential that children should be able to sleep at night..."

"But what's the sense of all this? For the Benefactor's sake, what's the sense of it, if everybody's happy as it is?"

"Let's assume everybody's happy. Very well, so be it, even. But what next?"

"That's ridiculous! A completely childish question. Tell something to children right to the end, and they'll be sure to ask, 'But what next? Why?'"

"Children are the only courageous philosophers. And courageous philosophers are invariably children. One should always be like a child. That's for certain. So what next?"

"There's nothing next! Period. It's evenly distributed all over the Universe, it's spread out everywhere..."

"Aha! Evenly distributed, everywhere! But that's just where you have entropy, psychological entropy. Surely it's clear to you, as a mathematician, that there are only differences: differences of temperature, heat contrasts; and only in them is there life. And if there are equally warm or equally cold bodies everywhere, all over the Universe, then they must be thrown into collision so that there will be fire, explosions, Gehenna. And we shall make them collide."

"But please, please understand that during the Two Hundred Years War, our ancestors did just that..."

"And they were right, a thousand times right. They only made one mistake:
they affirmed later that they were the last number—which simply does not exist in nature. Their mistake was also Galileo's: he was right about the Earth moving round the Sun, but he didn't know that the entire Solar System is moving round a centre; he didn't know that the real as distinct from the relative orbit of Earth is certainly not an elementary circle..."

"And you?"

"We know for the time being that there is no last number. Perhaps we shall forget. No, we shall surely forget when we grow old, just as when everything inevitably grows old. And then we too shall inevitably fall like the leaves from the trees in autumn, as you will the day after tomorrow... No, no, my dear, not you. You are with us, I know, you are with us!"

Flushed, excited, sparkling—I had never seen her like this before. She had embraced me, all of her, and I had disappeared...

She said her last words, looking me steadfastly and firmly in the eye.

"So remember—at twelve."

And I said:

"Yes, I remember."

She left. I was on my own amid the stormy, polyphonic din of dark-blue, red, green, bronze-yellow and orange...

Yes, at 12... Suddenly, I had an incongruous sensation that something extraneous had settled on my face, something that I could not get rid of in any way at all. Suddenly, yesterday morning, U, and what she had shouted in I-330's face. Why? How absurd!

I hastened to get outside and go home as quickly as possible.

Somewhere behind me I heard the harsh screeching of the birds over the Wall. In front of me, in the setting sun, from the mulberry-red crystallised fire rose the spheres of domes, the enormous flaming cubes of houses and, like lightning frozen in the sky, the spires of the accumulator towers. And all this flawless geometrical beauty I must myself, with my own hands... Was there really no way out, no other course?

I walked past one of the auditoriums (I don't remember its number). Inside, the benches had been piled up into heaps: in the middle were tables covered with sheets of snow-white glass; there was a patch of rose-red sunny blood on the white. Some kind of unknown and therefore sinister tomorrow was concealed in all this. It was unnatural for a thinking, seeing creature to live amid irregularities, unknowns, x's. As if I was being made to walk blindfold, feeling my way, stumbling, knowing that somewhere the brink was very near; only one step and nothing would be left of me but a squashed, mangled piece of meat. Wasn't that the same thing?

...But what if I didn't wait for it and simply dived down head-first? Wouldn't that be natural and right, the instant solution to it all?

Entry No. 31
Summary:

THE GREAT OPERATION.
I HAVE FORGIVEN ALL.
COLLISION OF TRAINS.

We're saved! At the very last moment, when it seemed there was nothing to clutch hold of, everything is finished...

As if you had already mounted the steps to the

192

terrible Benefactor's Machine and the glass hood had closed over you with a heavy clang, and for the last time in your life, hastily, you are gulping down the blue sky with your eyes...

And suddenly it's all a "dream". The sun is rosy and cheerful; and the wall—what a joy it is to stroke the cold surface with your hand; and the pillow—to feast your eyes endlessly on the depression left by your head in its white surface...

That is approximately what I experienced when I read the State Newspaper this morning. I'd had a terrible dream, but it had come to an end. And I, the pusillanimous, I, the unbeliever, I was already thinking of self-willed death. I feel ashamed when I read the last lines I wrote yesterday. But it doesn't matter: let them stay as they are, like a memory of the incredible that could have been but shall never be... No, shall never be!...

This was what shone on Page One of the State Newspaper:

"Rejoice,

Henceforth you are perfect! Until this day, your brainchildren, the machines were more perfect than you.

In what way?

Each spark in a dynamo is a spark of purest reason; each stroke of the piston is an immaculate syllogism. But does not that unerring reason abide in you too?

Philosophy in cranes, presses and pumps is as consummate and clear as a circle drawn by a pair

193

of dividers. But is your own philosophy less circular?

The beauty of a machine is in its rhythm, as unswerving and accurate as a pendulum. But have not you, nourished since childhood on the Taylor system, also become as precise as pendulums?

Only one thing:

Machines have no fantasy.

Have you ever seen a distant, meaninglessly dreamy smile spread over the face of a pump cylinder? Have you ever heard cranes in the night, during the hours of sleep, tossing and turning restlessly and sighing?

No!

But amongst you—and you may well blush for shame—the Guardfans have been seeing these smiles and sighs more and more frequently. And—cover your eyes—the historians of the Unified State are applying for retirement so as not to record these ignominious events.

But it is not your fault: you are ill. The name of this disease is

fantasy.

It is the worm gnawing the black wrinkles across your brow. It is the fever that drives you to run still further, even though this "further" began where happiness ended. It is the last barricade on the road to happiness.

Rejoice: it has already been blown up.

The road is open.

The latest discovery of State Science: the centre of fantasy is a pathetic brain node in the region of

the pons Varolii. A triple irradiation of this node with X-rays and you are cured of fantasy—
                                                    forever.

You are perfect, you are machine-equivalent, the road to one-hundred-percent happiness is open. Hurry, all of you, young and old, to undergo the Great Operation. Hurry to the Auditorium where the Great Operation will take place. Long live the Great Operation. Long live the Unified State, long live the Benefactor!"

If you were to read all this not in my notes, which resemble an ancient and eccentric novel; if you held, as I am doing now, this sheet of newspaper still smelling of ink in your shaky hands; if you knew, as I do, that all this is the most real reality, and if not today's, then certainly tomorrow's—wouldn't you feel exactly as I do? Wouldn't your head reel, like mine? Wouldn't those uncanny, sweet needles of ice run up and down your spine and your arms too? Would it not seem to you that you are a giant, you are Atlas, and if you stood up upright you would surely bang your head on the glass ceiling?

I snatched up the telephone.

"I-330... Yes, yes, 330." Then, choking, I shouted, "Are you at home? Have you read—you're reading it? Why, it's, it's... It's astounding!"

"Yes..." A long, dark silence. The earpiece was buzzing faintly, was thinking... "I must see you without fail today. Yes, at my place after sixteen. Without fail."

Darling! What a darling! "Without fail"... I felt myself smiling and couldn't stop, so I would take that smile with me along the street, like a torch held high over my head...

Outside, the wind assailed me. It spun me round, whistled, lashed. But I was only all the more cheerful. Howl, wail, it doesn't matter: you won't blow any walls over now. And overhead, the iron-grey clouds were tumbling down. Carry on: you won't blot out the sun: we have chained it to the zenith for all time, we, the Joshuas.

On the corner, a dense cluster of Joshuas were standing with their foreheads pressed up against the glass of the wall. Inside, a man was already lying on a dazzlingly white table. The bare soles of his feet, in the form of a yellow V, were protruding from under a white sheet, white medics were stooping over the head of the bed, and a white hand reached out to offer another hand a freshly charged syringe.

"Why don't you go too?" I asked no one in particular, or rather all of them.

"What about you?" Someone's spherical head turned to me.

"I'll go later. I have something to attend to first..."

The shipyard. *Integral*, pale-blue, was glittering and sparkling. The dynamo was buzzing in the engine-room, caressingly repeating a word over and over again as if it was a familiar word of my own.

I bent over and stroked the long, cold pipe of the engine. Dearest... What a darling! Tomorrow you'll come to life, tomorrow, for the first time, you'll shudder at the fiery spray in your womb...

With what eyes would I have looked at that mighty glass monster if all had remained as yesterday? If I had known that tomorrow, at 12, I would betray it... yes, betray it...

A hand grasped me cautiously by the elbow from behind. I looked round. It was the flat, plate-like face of the Second Constructor.

"You already know," he said.

"About what? The Operation? Yes, it's wonderful, isn't it? Everything suddenly becomes..."

"No, I didn't mean that. The test flight's been postponed until the day after tomorrow. All because of that Operation... They've been driving us hard to no purpose..."

"All because of that Operation"... Funny, limited man. Couldn't see further than the end of his nose. If only he knew that if it weren't for the Operation he'd be sitting under lock and key in a glass cage, he'd be throwing himself about in there and trying to climb up the wall...

My room at 15.30. I went in and saw U. She was sitting at my table, all skin and bones, erect, rigid, her right cheek propped up on her hand. She must have been waiting for a long time, because when she jumped up to meet me, the five depressions from her fingers were still visible on her cheek.

For a moment, I remembered that most unhappy morning, with her just here, near the table, in a fury, with I-330 present... But only for a moment, and it was all immediately washed away by the day's sunshine. Just as when, on a bright day, you go into a room and absent-mindedly turn the switch and the bulb lights up, but it's as if it wasn't there, it's so ridiculously pointless, faint and unnecessary...

Without thinking, I offered her my hand and forgave everything: she seized both my hands and gripped them with a prickly tightness and, her pendulous cheeks quivering agitatedly like ancient ornaments, she said:

"I've been waiting... I won't be a minute.. I only want to say how happy I am, how glad I am for you! Just think, tomorrow or the day after you'll be completely fit, you'll be born again..."

I saw a sheet of paper on the table, the last two pages of my notes for the previous day; they were lying where I had left them in the evening. If she had seen what I had written there... Anyway, it didn't matter: that was merely history now, it was absurdly far away, as through reversed binoculars...

"Yes," I said, "and, you know, I was just walking along the prospekt, and there was a man in front of me, and his shadow was on the roadway. You see, his shadow was shining. And it seemed to me—I'm convinced of it—that tomorrow there won't be any shadows at all, not from a single person, not from a single thing. The sun will shine through everything..."

Then she, tenderly and sternly:

"You're a fantasist! I wouldn't allow my schoolchildren to talk like that..."

And something about the children, how she took them all together, in a flock, to the Operation, and how they had to be tied down there, and how "to love, one must do so ruthlessly, yes, ruthlessly" and how she would, it seemed, finally make up her mind to...

She adjusted the blue-grey fabric between her knees, silently and quickly plastered me all over with a smile and went out.

Fortunately, the sun had not yet stopped today, the sun was racing onwards, it was already 16, I was knocking at the door and my heart was knocking too...

"Come in!"

Down on to the floor in front of her armchair, embracing her legs, my head flung back, looking into her eyes, into one and then into the other by turns and seeing myself wonderfully imprisoned in each...

But out there, on the other side of the wall, it was stormy; out there the clouds were becoming more and more like cast-iron. Let them! My head was overcrowded, brimming over with turbulent words, and I was flying, aloud, with the sun somewhere—no, now we knew where to, and after me came planets spouting flame and inhabited by fiery singing flowers, and planets that were mute and dark-blue, on which the rational rocks were combined into organised societies, planets that had achieved, like our own Earth, the summits of absolute, one-hundred-percent happiness...

And suddenly, from above me:

"Don't you think that a summit consists precisely of rocks combined into an organised society?"

And the triangle became more acute, more dark:

"And happiness... What of it? After all, desires are torture, isn't that so? And happiness is clearly when there are no more desires, not a single one... What a mistake, what a stupid prejudice, that to this very day we have put a plus sign before happiness, but, of course, a minus sign, a divine minus, before absolute happiness."

I remember muttering in confusion:

"Absolute zero is minus 273°..."

"Minus 273°—exactly. Rather cool, but does not that very fact prove that we are on the summit?"

As before, a long time ago, she was somehow speaking for me, or through me, developing my thoughts to their conclusion. There was something so uncanny about this that I couldn't bear it and, with an effort, dragged the word "no" out of myself.

"No," I said. "You ... you're joking..."

She laughed loudly, too loudly. Quickly, in the space of a second, she laughed to a kind of limit, then stumbled and fell down... A pause.

She stood up. She laid her hands on my shoulders. She looked at me long and hard. Then she drew me to her, and there was nothing but her sharp, hot lips.

"Goodbye!"

It came from far away, from above, and only reached me after perhaps one minute, perhaps two.

"What d'you mean, 'Goodbye'?"

"But you're ill, you've committed a crime because of me. Wasn't it agonising for you? But now there's going to be an Operation and you'll be cured of me. So it's goodbye."

"No!" I shouted.

A mercilessly sharp black triangle on the white.

"Why? Don't you want happiness?"

My mind was at sixes and sevens: two logical trains had collided and were mounting on top of one another, toppling over, breaking up...

"Well, I'm waiting—choose: the Operation and one-hundred-percent happiness, or..."

"I can't live without you, I mustn't be without you," I said, or merely thought—I don't know which, but she heard me.

"Yes, I know," she replied. And then, still keeping her hands on my shoulders and not taking her eyes off mine:

"Until tomorrow, then. Tomorrow, at twelve. You won't forget, will you?"

"No. Postponed for one day... The day after tomorrow..."

"So much the better for us. At twelve, the day after tomorrow..."

I walked along the twilit street. The wind was

spinning me round, bearing me onwards, driving me like a scrap of paper; chunks of cast-iron sky were flying, flying—they still had a day or two to fly through infinity... The unifas of people coming the other way brushed against me, but I walked on alone. It was clear to me that all were saved, but there was no salvation for me any more, / didn't want salvation...

Entry No. 32
Summary:
I DO NOT BELIEVE. TRACTORS. THE HUMAN SPLINTER.

Do you believe that you will die? Yes, man is mortal, I am a man, consequently... No, that's wrong: I know that you know this. But I'm asking you if you've ever happened to believe this, to believe it finally, not with your mind, but with your body, to feel that there will come a time when the fingers holding this very page will be yellow and ice-cold...

No, of course you don't believe it, and that's why you still haven't jumped from the tenth story on to the roadway, and that is why to this day you eat, turn over a page, shave, smile, write...

It's the same, yes, exactly the same with me today. I know that little black hand on the watch will crawl this way, downwards, on the way to midnight, will slowly climb back up again, will cross a final line and the incredible tomorrow will begin. I know this, but I still somehow can't believe it, or perhaps it seems to me that twenty-four hours are twenty-four years. And that's why I can still do something, hurry off somewhere, answer questions, climb up the gangway on to *Integral*. I still feel it rocking on the water, and I realise that I must seize hold of the handrail, and there is cold glass under my hand. I can see the transparent, living cranes bending their stork-like necks and stretching out their beaks, solici-tously and tenderly feeding *Integral* with terrible explosive food for the engines. Down below, on the river, I can clearly see the blue, wind-inflated water veins and nodes. Even so, it's all somehow very remote from me, external, flat as a drawing on a sheet of paper. And it's strange when the flat, drawn face of the Second Constructor suddenly says:

"Well, how much fuel are we taking for the engines? If we reckon three ... well, three and a half hours..."

In front of me, projected on to the drawing, is my hand holding a counter, a logarithmic dial and the number 15.

"Fifteen tons. But it would be better to take ... yes, it would be better to take a hundred..."

This is because I know that tomorrow— —

And I can see out of the corner of my eye that the hand holding the dial is beginning to tremble imperceptibly.

"A hundred. But why such a vast quantity?

203

That's enough for a week. No, not just a week—more!"

"There's no knowing..."

"I know..."

The wind whistles, the whole air is tightly packed to the very top with something invisible. I find it hard to breathe and hard to walk. With difficulty, slowly, without stopping for a second, the hand crawls round on the accumulator tower at the far end of the prospekt. The spire of the tower, enveloped in cloud, is a dull dark-blue in colour and is wailing hollowly; it is sucking up electricity. The trumpets of the Music Factory are wailing.

As always, in ranks of four. But the ranks are somehow unsteady and, perhaps because of the wind, are wavering and bending. More and more. Now they've collided with something on the corner, have surged back, have become a solid, frozen, tightly packed, fast-breathing mass, and are all suddenly craning their long necks, like geese.

"Look! No, look! Over there, quick!"

"Them! It's them!"

"...But I—on no account! On no account—I'd sooner stick my head into the Machine..."

"Shhh! Madman!..."

On the corner, in the auditorium, the door is wide open and out of it is coming a slow, cumbersome column of about fifty men. However, "men" is the wrong word: not legs, but heavy, cumbersome wheels being rotated by an unseen drive; not people, but human-shaped tractors. Over their heads, a white banner emblazoned with golden sun is fluttering in the wind and there is an inscription in the sun's rays: "We are the first! We have been operated on! All follow us!"

Slowly, irresistibly they have ploughed their way through the crowd, and if, instead of us, there was a wall in their way, or a tree, or a house, they would obviously plough through the wall, the tree or the house just the same, without stopping. They are now already in the middle of the prospekt. Arms linked, they have strung out into a line facing us. And we are waiting, a tense mass bristling with heads. Stretching our necks like geese. Clouds. The wind is whistling.

Suddenly, the left and right wings of the line close in on us, advance on us faster and faster, like a heavy vehicle going downhill, close in on us and drive us towards the wide-open door, through the door, inside...

Someone's piercing shriek:

"They're herding us in! Run for it!"

All make a dash for it. Near the wall itself are the still narrow, living gates, all are rushing that way, head-first—the heads instantly sharpen into wedges—and sharp elbows, ribs, shoulders, sides. Like a jet of water compressed by a fireman's hose, they fan outwards, and all round are fleeing, stamping feet, fluttering arms and unifas. A double-bent body like the letter S with transparent wing-ears flits momentarily across my field of vision and then vanishes into thin air, and I am alone amidst the split-second arms and legs, running...

Into an entrance for a breather, my back firmly up against the door, and a tiny human splinter is instantly driven up against me as if by the wind.

"All the time I... I've been following you... I don't want to, you must understand, I don't want to. I agree..."

Round, tiny hands on my sleeve, round blue eyes. It's O. And now she somehow slides down the wall and settles on the ground. She's curled up into a ball there on the cold steps, and I stand over her, stroking her head and her face—my hands are wet. It's as if I am very big and she is tiny, a tiny part of my own self. This is something entirely different from I-330 and I promptly imagine that the ancients might have felt something of the kind about their private children.

From below, through the hands covering her face, I just manage to hear:

"Every night, I... I can't bear the thought of it, them curing me... Every night, I'm alone, I think about it in the dark, what it's going to be like, how I'm going to live, knowing... But then I'll have nothing to live for, d'you understand? And it's your duty, it's your duty..."

An absurd feeling, but I am indeed convinced that I must. Awkward, because this duty of mine is yet one more crime. Absurd, because white cannot be black at the same time, duty and crime cannot coincide. Or there is neither black nor white in life, and colour depends only on the basic logical premise. And if the premise is that I have illegally got her with child...

"All right, only don't, don't..." I said. "You understand, I must take you to I-330—just as I then suggested that she..."

"Yes..." (softly, without taking her hands away from her face).

I helped her to her feet. And in silence, thinking our own different thoughts, or, perhaps, thinking about the same thing, we went along the darkening street, amid the dumb leaden houses through the stiff, lashing branches of the wind...

At one transparent, tense point, I heard", through the whistling of the wind, familiar footsteps slapping as if through puddles. I looked round at the turning and saw S amid the racing inverted clouds in the dull glass of the roadway. I immediately acquired erratically waving arms that were not my own and I loudly told O that tomorrow ... yes, tomorrow, *Integral* would make its first flight and it would be something absolutely unprecedented, marvellous and uncanny.

O stared at me in round-eyed amazement and at my loudly, meaninglessly whirling arms. I didn't allow her to say a word, I kept on talking and talking. But one thought was feverishly buzzing and hammering away inside me, separately, inwardly, so that only I could hear it: "I mustn't... I must find a way of somehow... I mustn't go to I-330 with him following behind us..."

Instead of turning left, I turned right. The bridge offered its humbly, servilely bent back to the three of us—myself, O, and, behind us, S. From the illuminated buildings on the opposite bank, lights were showering down into the water and breaking up into thousands of feverishly dancing sparks sprinkled with rapid white foam. The wind boomed like a rope-thick bass string stretched somewhere overhead. And through the bass, behind us all the time— —

The house I live in. O stopped at the door and was about to say something:

"No! You promised..."

But I didn't let her finish and hurriedly pushed her through the doorway inside, into the vestibule. Over the control desk were the familiar, agitatedly wobbling pendulous cheeks; around was a tight cluster of numbers, some kind of dispute, heads hanging over the second-floor balustrade, individuals running down. But that can come later... I quickly pulled O away into the opposite corner, sat down with my back to the wall (outside, on the other side of the wall, I had seen a dark, big-headed shadow gliding over the pavement) and took out my notebook.

O slowly settled down in her armchair as if her body was evaporating, melting under her unifa, leaving only the empty dress, and empty eyes, their blue emptiness drawing me in. Wearily:

"Why have you brought me here? Have you played a trick on me?"

"No... Not so loud! Look over there. Can you see it, through the wall?"

"Yes. A shadow."

"He follows me all the time... I can't stand it. You understand, I can't go. I shall write a note in a moment. Take it with you and leave on your own. He'll stay here, I know that much."

The inflated body stirred again under the unifa, the stomach rounded slightly and there was a scarcely discernible dawn glow on the cheeks.

I thrust a note into her cold fingers, squeezed her hand tight and drank from her dark-blue eyes for the last time.

"Goodbye! Perhaps some time again..."

She took her hand away. Bent over, she slowly left, took two steps, turned round suddenly and she was with me again. Her lips moved; her eyes, her lips, the whole of her was trying to say the same word over and over again, and there was such an anguished smile on her face, such pain...

Then she was a hunched human splinter in the doorway, and then a tiny shadow behind the wall, not looking round, walking faster and faster...

I went over to U's table. Agitated, furious, she inflated her gills and said:

"You understand, they all seem to have gone mad! That one's claiming he saw a naked man covered with wool near the Ancient House..."

A voice from the dense cluster of people that was bristling with heads:

"Yes. And I'm saying it again—I saw him, I did!"

"Well, how about that, eh? There's delirium for you!"

209

And she spoke the word "delirium" with such conviction and inflexibility that I wondered, "Isn't it actually a kind of delirium, all that's been happening to me and round me recently?"

But I glanced at my hairy hands and remembered, "There must be a drop of forest blood in you. Perhaps that's why..."

No, fortunately, not delirium. No, unfortunately, not delirium.

Entry No. 33
Summary:

(NO SUMMARY, IN HASTE, THE LAST.)

The day has come.

The newspaper, quickly: perhaps it's in there... I read it with my eyes (exactly: my eyes are now like a pen, like a counter that you hold and feel in your hand; they're something outside of me, they're a tool).

There it is, in big lettering all over Page One.

"The enemies of happiness are not asleep. Hold on to happiness with both hands! Tomorrow, all work will temporarily be halted: all numbers will report for the Operation. Those who fail to appear will be subject to the Benefactor's Machine."

210

Tomorrow! Can it be so? Can there be some kind of tomorrow?

Out of daily inertia, I stretched my hand (tool) towards the bookshelf, to put the day's newspaper in a gilt-engraved binder with the rest. And as I was doing so:

"Why? Does it make any difference? After all, here, into this room, I shall never again, never..."

The newspaper fell from my hands on to the floor. I stood and looked round at the room, at all, all, all of it, and hastily collected up and feverishly crammed into an invisible suitcase everything that I was sorry to leave behind. The desk. The books. The armchair. I-330 had once sat on that chair, and I had been below, on the floor... The bed...

Then for a minute or two I foolishly waited for a miracle: perhaps the telephone would ring, perhaps she'd say that...

No. No miracle.

I am going away into the unknown. These are my last lines. Goodbye, unknown ones, loved ones with whom I suffered so many pages, to whom I, being sick in soul, revealed my whole self down to the last crushed screw, down to the last broken spring.

I'm going away.

Summary:

FREEDMEN. SUNNY NIGHT. RADIO-VALKYRIE.

Oh, if I had really smashed myself and everybody else into pieces, if only I had really, together with her, shown up somewhere behind the Wall in the midst of the beasts baring their yellow fangs, 'if only I had really never come back here again. It would be a thousand, a million times easier. But now what? Go and stifle that woman? But would that help in any way?

No, no, no! Take yourself in hand, D-503. Set yourself on a firm logical axis, press with all your might on the lever even if only for a short time and, like an ancient slave, turn the grindstones of syllogisms until you have recorded and interpreted everything that has happened...

When I went aboard *Integral*, all were already assembled, all were in their places, all the cells of the gigantic glass beehive were full. Through the glass of the decks could be seen the tiny ant-people below, near the telegraphs, the dynamos, the transformers, the altimeters, the valves, the pointers, the engines, the pumps, the pipes. In the wardroom, some people, presumably on assignment from the Science Bureau, were bent over tables and tools. And near them was the Second Constructor with two of his assistants.

All three had pulled their heads in between

their shoulders like tortoises, and their eyes were grey, autumnal, lustreless.

"Well?" I asked.

"A bit weird..." said one of them with a grey, lack-lustre smile. "We may have to go down no one knows where. No one knows anything at all..."

I found it intolerable to look at them, these men whom I was going to throw out with my own hands in an hour's time from the cosy figures of the Hour Tablet, whom I was going to wean from the maternal bosom of the Unified State. They reminded me of the tragic images of "The Three Freedmen", whose story is known to every schoolboy here. It tells how three numbers, in the interests of experience and experiment, were released from work for a month. "Do what you want and go where you like"[1]. The poor wretches loitered outside their usual place of work and stared inside with hungry eyes. They stayed on the squares and for whole hours at a time carried out the movements which had become necessary to their organisms at a certain time of day: they sawed or planed the air, banged away with invisible hammers and thumped invisible blanks. Finally, on the tenth day, they couldn't hold out any longer: they held one another's hands, walked into the water and, to the sounds of the March, sank deeper and

[1] This was a long time ago, in the 3rd Century after the Tablet.

deeper until the water put an end to their torment...

I repeat, I found it hard to look at them and I hastened to get away.

"I'm just going to make a check in the engine-room," I said, "and then off we go."

They asked me about something or other—what voltage to use for the launch explosion, how much water ballast should be put into the stern tank. There was a kind of gramophone inside me: it answered all the questions quickly and precisely and, without stopping, I continued thinking my own thoughts.

Suddenly, in a small passage, I glimpsed grey unifas and grey faces flitting past me, and among them, for a second, one with hair plastered down low over his forehead—him again. I realised that they were here, I would never get away from all this and there were only a few minutes—a few tens of minutes... An infinitesimally fine molecular tremor ran all over my body (it never stopped until the very end), as if an enormous engine had been installed in it, the housing of my body was too light for it and all the walls, partitions, cables, beams and lights were trembling...

I didn't yet know whether she was there. But there was no time now; a messenger was sent to call me back up again as quickly as possible to the control cabin: it was time to go... But where?

Grey, lacklustre faces. Tightly sprung dark-blue veins below, on the water. Heavy cast-iron layers of sky. And, as if of cast-iron myself, I lifted up the commander's telephone.

"Up—45°!"

A muffled explosion—a jolt—a frenzied white-and-green mountain of water in the stern—deck going away underfoot—soft, rubbery—and everything's down below, all life, forever... For a moment—falling deeper and deeper into a kind of crater, everything around shrinking—the bulging, ice-blue outlines of the city, the round bubbles of domes, the solitary leaden finger of the accumulator tower. Then a momentary cotton-wool curtain of cloud—we fly through it—and then the sun and the blue sky. Seconds, minutes, miles—the dark-blue is rapidly solidifying, is being filled with darkness, and the stars come out like drops of cold, silvery sweat.

And now an eerie, intolerably bright, black, starry solar night. What would it be like if you suddenly went deaf? You would still see the pipes roaring, but you would only see them: they would be mute, there would be silence. The sun was like that—mute.

It was natural, it was only to be expected. We had emerged from the Earth's atmosphere. But somehow it was so sudden, it was so unexpected that all those round me were cowed and fell silent. But I even felt more at my ease under that fantastic, mute sun as if, after my last convulsion, I had stepped across the inevitable threshold, my body was somewhere down below, and I was being

215

borne along in a new world where it was right that everything should be unfamiliar and upside down...

"Carry on!" I shouted into the telephone—or rather not I, but that gramophone inside me, and, with a mechanical, jointed arm, I pushed the speaking-tube to the Second Constructor. But I was clad from head to foot in a fine molecular tremor that only I could hear, and I hurried below to search...

The door to the wardroom, that same door; it would shut with a heavy clang in an hour's time... Near it was someone unfamiliar to me—short, with a face like that of a hundred, a thousand others and indistinguishable in a crowd, except that his arms were unusually long, reaching down to his knees, as if they had been taken in error from a different human assembly kit.

A long arm reached out and barred my way.

"Where to?"

He obviously didn't know that I knew everything. So be it: perhaps that was the way it ought to be. And I, towering over him, with deliberate abruptness:

"I am the Constructor of *Integral*. I am in charge of the tests. You understand?"

The arm was gone.

The wardroom. Over the instruments, maps—heads covered with grey stubble, and yellow, bald, ripe heads. All quickly bunch together, one look, and they go back, along the corridor and down the companionway into the engine-room. There is heat and thunder in there from pipes turned red-hot by the blasts, crankshafts glitter in a frenzied, drunken Cossack dance and needles quiver on dials in an almost indiscernible tremor that never stops for a moment.

And here, at last, near the tachometer, the man with his brow bulging low over a notebook...

"Listen... (thunder: I have to shout into his ear). Is she here? Where is she?"

In the darkness, a smile from under the brows.

"She? Over there. In the radio-telephone cabin..."

I go in. There are three of them inside. All are in winged earphone helmets. She seems to be a head taller than usual, winged, glittering, flying—like one of the ancient Valkyries; and it's as if there are enormous blue sparks on top, on the radio mast, and they're coming from her, and a faint, lightning-flash fragrance of ozone is also coming from her.

"Someone... No, at least you..." I said to her, out of breath (with running). "I have to send a message down, to Earth, to the shipyard... Let's go and I'll dictate it..."

Next to the apparatus room there is a tiny box of a cabin. We sit down at the table, side by side. I find her hand and grip it tight.

"Well, what now? What's going to happen?"

"I don't know. You understand how wonderful this is: to fly without knowing where; it just doesn't matter... And it will soon be twelve, and we don't know what's going to happen. And night... Where will you and I be in the night? Perhaps on grass, on dry leaves..."

Blue sparks are coming from her and there is a whiff of lightning, and my internal tremor is even worse.

"Write down." I say loudly and still out of breath (with running). "Time—eleven thirty. Speed—six thousand eight hundred..."

She, softly, from under the winged helmet, without taking her eyes off the paper:

"She came to me with your note yesterday... I know, I know all about it; don't say anything. But the child is yours, isn't it? I sent her there; she's already behind the Wall. She will live..."

I am back in the control cabin. Another delirious night with a black starry sky and a blinding sun. The hand of the clock on the wall limps slowly across one minute to the next. Everything is as in a mist and clad in a very fine, almost imperceptible (except to me) tremor.

For some reason, I decided that it would be better for everything to happen not here, but somewhere down below, closer to Earth.

"Stop!" I shouted into the machine.

Forward movement continuing, by inertia, but more and more slowly. And now *Integral* caught on a kind of split-second hair, hung motionless briefly, then the hair snapped and *Integral* dropped like a stone, faster and faster. And so in silence, minutes, tens of minutes, I could hear my own pulse, the hands before my eyes were moving closer and closer to 12, and it was clear to me

218

that I was a stone and she was the Earth; but I was a stone thrown by someone, and the stone is intolerably eager to fall to the ground and be smashed to pieces... But what if?.. Down below was the solid, dark-blue smoke of clouds... But what if?..

But the gramophone in me picked up the speaking-tube neatly, as if hinged, ordered "Slow", and the stone stopped falling. Only the four lower nozzles were snorting wearily, two in the bows and two in the stern, solely to nullify the weight of *Integral*. Trembling slightly, the ship stopped as securely as if at anchor about a kilometre above the surface.

All streamed out on to the deck (it was now 12, the bell was ringing for dinner) and, bending over the glass rail, hastily gulped in the unknown world outside that lay there down below. Amber, green, blue: an autumnal wood, meadow, a lake. On the edge of the dark-blue saucer of a lake there were yellow, bone-like ruins and a threatening, shrivelled yellow finger; it must have been the miraculously preserved tower of an ancient church.

"Look, look! Over there, to the right!"

A swift blob was flying like a brown shadow over the green wilderness. I was holding a pair of binoculars, so I automatically raised them to my eyes. A herd of brown horses, their tails lashing, was galloping chest-high through the grasses, and mounted on them were those people—dark-bay, white, raven-black...

Behind me:

"I'm telling you, I saw it, a face."

"Come off it. Tell me another!"

"All right, then, here, take the binoculars..."

But they had already disappeared. Just the endless green wilderness...

And, in the wilderness, filling all of it and all of me and everybody else, the shrilling of the dinner-bell. One minute to go before 12.

The world broken up into momentary, disjointed fragments. Someone's gold plaque ringing on the companionway steps, but I didn't care, and it crunched under my heel. A voice: "But I tell you, a face!" A dark rectangle: the open door of the wardroom. Tightly clenched, white, sharply smiling teeth...

And at the very moment when, with infinite slowness, without taking a breath between one stroke and the next, the clock began to strike and the front rows already moved off, the rectangle of the door was suddenly blocked by two familiar, unnaturally long arms.

"Stop!"

Fingers dug into my palm. It was I-330, at my side.

"Who's that? D'you know him?"

"But surely ... surely..."

He towered over the rest of us. Over hundred of faces, his was one in a hundred, one in a thousand, the only face amongst them all.

"In the name of the Guardians... To you—whom I am addressing, they can hear, each of them can hear me—to you I say: we know. We do not know your numbers yet, but we know everything. *Integral* shall not be yours! The test will be carried to its conclusion, but as for you—you shall not dare to move now—as for you, you shall do this with your own hands. And then... But I have finished..."

Silence. The glass slabs underfoot are soft, are cotton-wool, and I have soft, cotton-wool legs. Beside me is her perfectly white smile and frenzied, dark-blue sparks. Through clenched teeth, into my ear:

"So it's you, is it? You've 'fulfilled your duty'? Very well, then..."

Her hand had torn itself out of mine and the Valkyrie's wrathfully winged helmet was somewhere far in front. On my own, frozen wid speechless like everybody else, I went into the wardroom...

"But it wasn't me, it wasn't me at all! I never said a word about it to anybody except for these dumb white pages!.."

Inside myself, inaudibly, desperately, loudly, I was shouting this at her. She was sitting opposite at the table and she did not even once touch me with her eyes. Beside her was someone's yellow-ripe bald head. I could hear her voice:

"'Nobility'? But my dear professor, even a simple philological analysis of the word shows that it is a prejudice, a left-over from the ancients, from feudal times. But we..."

I felt myself turning pale, and soon everybody would notice... But the gramophone in me was executing the 50 stipulated masticatory motions per bite. I locked myself inside myself, as in an ancient opaque house; I barricaded the door with stones and I drew the curtains across the windows...

Then I was holding the speaking-tube in my hand, and flight—in icy, ultimate despair, through the clouds into the icy, sun-starred night. Minutes, hours. And, apparently, all this time, everything in me was going feverishly, at full speed—I myself could not hear the logical engine. Because suddenly, at a certain point in dark-blue space, I saw my writing desk, the gill-like cheeks of U over it, and the sheet of notes about which I had forgotten. And I realised that no one but her—I realised it all too clearly...

Oh, if only I could get to the radio... Winged helmets, the tang of dark-blue lightning flashes... I remember saying something loudly to her and I remember her looking through me from afar, as if I was glass:

"I'm busy. I'm receiving from below. Dictate it to her over there..."

In the tiny box-cabin, after a moment's thought, I firmly dictated:

"Time—fourteen-fourty. Down! Stop engines. It's all over."

The control cabin. The engine heart of *Integral* had stopped, we were falling, but my heart was too late to fall, it was lagging behind, it was rising higher and higher to my throat... Clouds, and then, in the distance, a green blob becoming

222

greener and greener, more and more prominent, rushing at us like a tornado—the end was near— —

The porcelain-white and contorted face of the Second Constructor. It must have been he who pushed me with all his strength so that I hit my head on something and, blacking out as I fell, heard indistinctly:

"Stern engines, full speed ahead!"

A violent upward lurch... I don't remember any more.

Entry No. 35
Summary:

IN A HOOP. THE CARROT. MURDER.

I couldn't sleep all night. My mind was on one thing all the time...

My head was tightly bandaged after yesterday's blow. Except that it wasn't a bandage, it was a hoop. Merciless, made of glass steel, that hoop was rivetted on to my head and I was trapped in one and the same forged iron circle: to kill U. To kill U and then go to the other one and say, "Now d'you believe me?" The most disgusting thing of all is that killing is somehow dirty and old-fashioned: the idea of braining someone leaves a strange sensation of something revoltingly sweet in the mouth, and I couldn't swallow my own saliva; I was spitting it out into a handkerchief all the time and my mouth was dry.

I had in my cupboard a heavy piston-rod that had broken after casting (I had to study the structure of the fracture under the microscope). I rolled up my notes (let her read all of me, to the last letter), pushed a piece of the rod inside them and went downstairs. The stairs were endless, each step was revoltingly soft and slippery, and I had to keep wiping my mouth with my handkerchief all the time...

Down below. My heart thudded. I stopped. I took out the rod and went to the control desk— —

U wasn't there: an empty, icy desk. Then I remembered that all work had been cancelled, everybody had to go for the Operation. That made sense: there was no point in her being there, since there was no one to put down in the register...

Outside. Wind. A sky of racing cast-iron slabs. And, as at a certain moment yesterday, the whole world was smashed into separate, sharp, independent fragments, and each of them was falling headlong, stopping for a moment, hanging in mid-air in front of me and then evaporating without a trace.

What would it be like if the black, precise letters on this page suddenly left their places and, in terror, rushed off in different directions so that there was not a single coherent word, just nonsense, balderdash? Well, the crowd on the street was like that, scattered, not in their ranks any more but rushing back, slantwise, criss-cross...

No one left. And for a brief moment, headlong, all froze. Up above on the second floor, in a glass cell suspended in mid-air, were a man and a woman, both standing up and kissing, her whole body bent limply backwards. It was forever, it was the last time...

In a corner, a stirring, prickly bush of heads. Over the heads, detached, in the air, a banner inscribed "Down with the Machines! Down with the Operation!" And separately (from me), I thought in a split-second: "Does everyone indeed have the kind of pain that can be torn out from inside only with the heart, and must something be done to each before— —?" And, for a second, nothing in the whole world except (my) animal hand with the cast-iron-heavy roll...

Then there was a little boy, the whole of him straining forward, with a shadow under his lower lip. That lower lip was turned back like the cuff of an upthrust sleeve. His whole face was turned inside-out. He was bawling and fleeing from someone as fast as he could, with the trample of feet behind him.

From the little boy: 'Yes, U must be in school now, you'll have to hurry." I ran to the nearest entrance to the underground.

Someone hurrying out of the doorway:

"They're not running! The trains aren't running today! Down there it's—"

I went below. It was an absolute nightmare

down there. The glitter of faceted crystal suns. The platform firmly tamped down with heads. An empty, motionless train.

And, in the silence, a voice. Hers. I couldn't see her, but I knew it, I knew that resilient, flexible, whiplash voice, and somewhere there would be a sharp triangle of brows tilted up towards the temples...

"Let me through! Let me through! I've got to—"

But someone's hands gripped me like pincers by the arms and shoulders, like nails. And a voice in the silence:

"No, run back up again! They'll cure you up there, they'll feed you on rich happiness, and, filled to satiety, you will peacefully sleep in an organised manner, in tempo, snoring. Can you not hear that great symphony of snores? You are comical; they want to liberate you from the question-marks that writhe like worms, that gnaw agonisingly, like worms. But you are standing here and listening to me. Go back up again, as quickly as possible, to the Great Operation! What's it to you that I shall be left here alone? What's it to you if I don't want others to want on my behalf, if I want to do my own wanting, if I want the impossible..."

Another voice, slow and heavy:

"Aha! The impossible? That means, chase after your foolish fantasies, so that they should wriggle their tails right in front of your nose? No, we are for the tail, under ourselves, and then..."

"But then you'll gobble them up, you'll start snoring, and you'll need a new tail under your nose. They say the ancients had an animal called the ass. To make it keep going forward all the time, they tied a carrot to the shafts in front of its nose so that the animal couldn't actually reach it. And if it did, the ass gobbled it up..."

Suddenly, the pincers released me, I rushed into the centre where she was talking, and at that very moment the people all began scattering and crowding together, and there was a shout from behind: "They're coming this way, they're coming!" The light jumped and went out—someone had cut the cable. An avalanche, shouts, wheezing, heads, fingers...

I don't know how much time we spent slithering about in the underground tunnel. Finally, there were steps, a dim light getting brighter and brighter, and then we were in the street again, fanning out in different directions...

And then I was alone. A wind, with grey, low clouds only just overhead. Dusk. On the wet glass of the pavement, deep down below, the lights and walls were inverted and inverted human figures were moving their legs. And that incredibly heavy roll in my hand, dragging me right down towards the bottom.

Downstairs, U was still missing from her desk and her room was empty and dark.

I went up to my own place and put on the light. My temples were throbbing, tightly bound by a hoop, and I walked about, locked all the time in one and the same circle: the desk, the white roll on the desk, the bed, the door, the desk, the white roll... The blinds of the room on the left had been lowered... On the right, over a book—a bumpy bald patch and the enormous yellow parabola of a forehead. The wrinkles on it were a row of yellow, indecipherable lines. Sometimes our eyes would meet, and then I would feel that those yellow lines were about me.

...It happened at 21 precisely. U arrived, in person. Only one thing is still clear in my memory: my breathing was so noisy that I could hear it myself and I wanted to quieten it down somehow, but failed.

She sat down and straightened the unifa on her knees. The rosy brown gills were quivering.

"Oh, my dear, so it's true that you've been hurt? The moment I found out about it, I immediately..."

The piston-rod was on the table in front of me. I jumped up, breathing even more loudly. She heard, stopped in mid-word and also stood up for some reason. I could already see that place on her head, there was a revolting sweetness in my mouth... Hankie, but I hadn't got one, so I spat on to the floor.

The man behind the wall on the right—yellow, intent wrinkles, and all about me. He mustn't see, and it would be even more disgusting if he was watching... I pressed the button. What if I had no right to do so? It hardly mattered now. The blinds came down.

She evidently sensed something, understood and made a dash for the door. But I beat her to it, breathing heavily and not for a second taking my eyes off that place on her head...

"You ... you've gone mad! You daren't..." She backed away and sat, or rather fell on to the bed and, trembling, thrust the clasped palms of her hands between her knees. Taut as a spring and still holding her tightly on a leash with my eyes, I slowly reached out to the table—only my hand moved—and seized hold of the piston-rod.

"I beg you! A day, only one day! Tomorrow, really tomorrow, I'll go and do everything..."

What did she mean? I swung back the piston-rod— —

And I consider that I killed her. Yes, you, my unknown readers, have the right to call me a murderer. I know that I would have brought the piston-rod down on her head if she hadn't screamed, "For the sake ... for the sake of... I agree, I ... now."

With shaking hands she tore off her unifa, and the spacious, yellow, pendulous body collapsed on to the bed... Only now did I realise it: she thought I had dropped the blinds so as to ... because I wanted...

It was so unexpected, so ludicrous that I burst out laughing. The tightly coiled spring inside me snapped, my hand weakened and the piston-rod crashed to the floor. I now knew from my own experience that laughter is the deadliest weapon of all: with laughter you can murder anything, even murder.

I sat at the desk laughing—desperate, final laughter—and could see no way out of the whole grotesque situation. I don't know how it would have ended if it had taken its normal course, but suddenly there was a new external additive: the telephone started ringing.

I rushed to grip the receiver. Was it her, perhaps? An unfamiliar voice in the earpiece:

"Now."

A tiresome, endless buzzing. From a long way away, heavy footsteps coming nearer, and sounding more and more resonant, more cast-iron. And then this:

"D-503? Ahem... This is the Benefactor. Come and see me immediately!"

Beep! The other end had hung up. Beep!

U was still lying on the bed, her eyes closed, her gills expanded widely in a smile. I raked her dress up off the floor, threw it over her and said through clenched teeth:

"Come on! Hurry up, hurry up!"

She half-raised herself on one elbow, her breasts flopped sideways, her eyes were round, she was like a wax dummy.

"What d'you mean?"

"I mean get dressed!"

All hunched up and tightly clutching her unifa, she said in a squashed voice:

"Turn your back..."

I turned away and rested my head on the glass. Lights, human shapes and sparks were trembling in the black, wet mirror. No: this was me, this was in me... What did He want me for? Did He know about her already, and about me, and about everything else?

U, dressed by now, was at the door. I took two steps towards her and gripped her hands as if to squeeze out of them, drop by drop, everything that I needed.

"Listen... Her name—you know whom I mean—you mentioned her name, didn't you? No? Only the truth, it's important to me; only the truth..."

"No."

"No? But why—since you've already been there and reported..."

Her lower lip was suddenly turned inside out, like that little boy's, and tears were coming out of her cheeks and trickling down them...

"Because I... I was afraid that if she ... that you might... you might stop lov— Oh, I just can't—I wouldn't have been able!"

"I understand. That's the truth. The stupid, ridiculous human truth!" I opened the door.

231

Entry No. 36
Summary:
EMPTY PAGES. THE CHRISTIAN GOD. ABOUT MY MOTHER.

It's strange here: my head is as blank as a white sheet of paper: I remember nothing of how I went there, how I waited (I know I waited), I can't remember a single sound, a single face, a single gesture. As if all the lines between me and the world had been cut.

When I came to I was already standing before Him, and I was terrified to look up: I could only see the enormous, cast-iron hands on His knees. He Himself was weighed down by His hands, His knees giving out. He was slowly moving his fingers. His face was somewhere in a mist up above, and it was as if it was only because His voice was coming down to me from such a height that it didn't boom like thunder and didn't deafen me, but was still like an ordinary human voice.

"And so you too? You, the Constructor of *Integral*? You, the one who was destined to be a great conquistador? You, whose name was to have opened a new and brilliant chapter in the history of the Unified State?.. You?"

The blood rushed to my head, into my cheeks. Again, a blank page, but a pulse was throbbing in my temples; there was a resounding voice booming

232

above me, but not a single word. Only when he stopped speaking did I come to myself and see the hand stir as if it weighed a hundred pounds; it started moving slowly in my direction and a finger pointed fixedly at me.

"Well? Have you nothing to say? Yes or no? The executioner?"

"Yes," I answered submissively. After that, I distinctly heard His every word.

"What? Do you think I fear this word? But have you ever tried to tear the husk off it and see what was inside? I will show you now. Remember, a dark-blue hill, a cross, a crowd. Some, up above, bespattered with blood, are nailing a body to a cross; others, below, bespattered with tears, are looking on. Don't you think that the role of those up there was the most difficult, the most important? Had it not been for them, would all this majestic tragedy ever have been staged? They were booed by the ignorant mob; but the author of the tragedy, God, had to reward them even more generously for this. But that same Christian and most merciful God, slowly burning all the unsubmissive ones in the flames of Hell, was He not really an Executioner? And were there really fewer burned at the stake by the Christians than there were Christians burned? And yet—understand this—and yet this God was glorified for centuries as the God of love. An absurdity? No, on the contrary: a patent, written in blood, on the ineradicable wisdom of man. Even then, though a hairy savage, he understood that the true, algebraic love for humanity, the invariable sign of the truth, is its cruelty. As with fire, the invariable sign is that it burns. Will you show me a fire that does not burn? Come on, prove it, dispute it!"

How could I argue? How could I argue when these had (formerly) been my own ideas, except that I had never been able to clothe them in such well-forged, shining armour. I said nothing...

"If this means that you agree with me, then let us talk like adults when the children have gone to bed: without constraint. I ask you—for what have people prayed, dreamed and suffered ever since they were in swaddling clothes? For someone to tell them once and for all what happiness is and then shackle them to that happiness. What are we doing now if not just that? The ancient dream of paradise... Remember, in paradise they no longer have desires, they do not know pity, they do not know love, those blessed angels, the slaves of God, who have had their fantasy removed by operation (which is the only reason why they are blessed)... And behold, at the very moment when we have already achieved that dream, when we seized hold of it like this (His hand tightened, and if there had been a stone in it, water would have spurted out of that stone), when all that remained was to gut the prey and divide it up into pieces, at that precise moment, you, you..."

The cast-iron booming suddenly stopped. I was red all over, like a workpiece on the anvil under a crashing hammer. The hammer was hanging silent over me, and to wait—it was even more terr...

Suddenly:

"How old are you?"

"Thirty-two."

"Exactly double—and the naively of a sixteen-year-old! Listen, did it really never enter your head even once that they—we don't know their names yet, but I am convinced we'll find out from you—that they only needed you as the Constructor of *Integral*—only so that through you..."

"Stop! Stop!" I exclaimed.

...You might just as well shield yourself with your hands and shout that at a bullet: you can still hear your own ridiculous 'Stop!', but the bullet has already gone through you and you're writhing on the floor.

Yes, yes, the Constructor of *Integral*... Yes, yes ... and, immediately, U's face, infuriated, with the quivering, brick-red gills—that morning when both women were in my room...

I remember very clearly that I burst out laughing and raised my eyes. A man as bald as Socrates was sitting in front of me and his head was bedewed with fine drops of perspiration.

How simple everything is. How majestically banal and simple to the point of absurdity.

My laughter was stifling me, was bursting out of me like puffs of smoke. I covered my mouth with the palm of my hand and rushed headlong out of the place.

Steps, wind, damp, dancing fragments of lights,

of faces, and, as I ran: "No! I must see her! I must see her just once more!"

And now another blank white page. I remember only feet. Not people, just feet: stamping raggedly, falling from somewhere above on to the roadway, hundreds of feet, a heavy rain of feet. And a kind of cheerful, frisky song, and a shout—perhaps meant for me: "Hey, hey! This way, come and join us!"

Then a deserted square, packed tight with a stiff breeze. In the middle, the dull, cumbersome, ominous mass of the Benefactor's Machine. And an unexpected echo from it inside me: a brilliantly white pillow, and on it a head thrown back with half-closed eyes: a sharp, sweet row of teeth... And all this was somehow incongruously and horribly connected with the Machine—I knew how, but I didn't want to see any more, to name it out loud—I didn't want to, I mustn't.

I closed my eyes and sat down on the steps leading up to the Machine. It must have been raining; my face was damp. Somewhere far away there was a muffled screaming. But no one could hear, no one could hear me screaming, "Save me from that, save me!"

Would that I might have a mother, like the ancients: a mother of my own, truly of my own. And would that to her I should be not the Constructor of *Integral*, not Number D-503, not a molecule of the Unified State, but a simple piece of humanity, a piece of her,—trampled on, crushed, cast out...

And let me nail up or be nailed—perhaps it's one and the same thing—so that she might hear what no one hears, so that her senile lips, overgrown with wrinkles—

INFUSORIA. DOOMSDAY.
HER ROOM.

Morning in the dining-room. The man on my left whispered to me in fright:

"Come on, eat! They're staring at you!"

I smiled with all my might. And it felt like a crack in my face: I was smiling, the edges of the crack were flying further and further apart and I was finding it more and more painful...

And then: no sooner had I speared a cube on my fork than the fork immediately trembled in my hand and rattled against the plate—the tables shuddered and rang, and so did the walls, the crockery, the air; outside, there was an enormous iron, round booming all the way up to the sky, and it went over heads, over buildings and died far away in small, almost indiscernible rings, as on water.

I saw faces instantly faded and drained of all colour, mouths stopped at full speed, forks stilled in mid-air.

237

Then everything became confused and went off the centuries-old rails. All jumped up from their places (without singing the anthem) any old how, not in rhythm, finishing their mouthfuls, choking, crowding together and clutching at one another. "What is it? What's happened? What is it?" And the disordered fragments of the once harmonious great Machine all streamed downwards to the lifts, down the stairs—steps, tramping feet, bits of words like the scraps of a letter torn up and whirled away by the wind...

They were likewise streaming out of all the neighbouring buildings, and very soon the prospekt was like a drop of water under the microscope: the infusoria locked in the transparent glass drop were rushing distractly to the sides, upwards, downwards.

"Aha," said a triumphant voice. In front of me was the back of someone's head and a finger pointing up at the sky. I can very clearly remember the yellow-and-pink fingernail and, below the nail, a white crescent like the moon rising from behind the horizon. It was like a compass: hundreds of eyes followed that finger and turned skywards.

Up there, in flight from an invisible pursuit, the clouds were speeding, crushing one another, leaping over one another, and then, painted with clouds, the dark aeros of the Guardians with the black trunks of hoses dangling down, and then, still further away, in the west, something that resembled— —

At first, no one understood what it was. Even I didn't understand, although (unfortunately) it was more obvious to me than to anyone else. It was like an enormous swarm of black aeros: scarcely discernible swift dots at an incredible altitude. They drew nearer and nearer, hoarse, guttural drops falling from above until they were over our heads—birds. They filled the sky with sharp, black, piercing, falling triangles; they were as if storm-driven, settling on domes, on roofs, on telegraph poles, on balconies.

"Aha-a!" The triumphant back of the head turned round and I saw the one with the bulging forehead. But all that remained of him now was a kind of book title; all of him had somehow crawled out of the eternal underbrow, and on his face, near the eyes and near the lips, rays were growing in tufts of hair. He was smiling.

"D'you understand?" he shouted to me through the whistle of the wind and the wings, through all the croaking. "D'you understand? The Wall, they've blown up the Wall! Un-der-sta-a-nd?"

Somewhere in the background, human figures were flitting past, heads outstretched, running into the houses as fast as they could, indoors. Down the middle of the roadway, a swift and yet somehow slow (because of its weight) avalanche of Operation victims, marching yonder, westwards.

Hairy clusters of rays near the lips and eyes. I clutched him by the arm.

"Listen, where is she? Where's I-330? Over

there, behind the Wall, or...? I must—d'you hear? At once, I can't stand it..."

"She's here!" he shouted drunkenly, merrily—strong yellow teeth... "She's here, in the city, she's taking action. Oh yes, we're taking action!"

Who were we? Who was I?

Close by there were about fifty like him: noisy, cheerful and with strong teeth, they had crawled out from under their beetling brows. Gulping down the storm with wide-open mouths, brandishing such apparently innocuous and unterrifying electrocutors (where had they obtained them?), they moved off in the same direction, westwards, in the wake of the Operation victims, but outflanking them along the parallel 48th Prospekt...

Stumbling over tight ropes of wind, I ran towards her. Why? I don't know. I kept tripping up; empty streets, an alien, savage city, the incessant, triumphant din of the birds, the end of the world. Through the glass of the walls in several houses I saw (it sticks in my memory) the figures of men and women coupling shamelessly without even having lowered the blinds, without tickets, in broad daylight...

The house, her house. The door disconcertingly ajar. No one at the control desk downstairs. The lift stuck halfway up the shaft. Gasping for breath, I ran up endless stairs. The corridor. Quickly, like wheel-spokes, the numbers on the doors: 320, 326 ... I-330, yes!

I could see through the glass door that everything in the room had been scattered about, overturned, crumpled up. A hastily overturned chair, supine, all four legs in the air, like a dead animal. The bed had been pointlessly shifted at an angle away from the wall. On the floor lay the fallen, trampled-on petals of rose-red tickets.

I bent over and picked up one, a second, a third: all had D-503 on them. I was on every one, a drop of me that had melted and spilled over the brim. They were all that was left...

For some reason, I couldn't let them lie there like that on the floor to be trodden on. I picked up another handful and put them on the table, smoothed them out carefully, looked and—burst out laughing.

I hadn't known it before, but I do now, and so do you: laughter comes in various colours. This is only a remote echo of an explosion within: perhaps it is festive, red, dark-blue, gold rockets, perhaps bits of a human body flying up into the air...

I glimpsed a totally unfamiliar name on the tickets. I can't remember the number, only the letter, which was F. I swept all the tickets off the table on to the floor, stepped on them—it was just like stepping on myself with my own heel—and went out...

I sat on the window-sill in the corridor opposite the door, waiting for something, obtusely, for a long time. Footsteps began slapping along on the left. It was an old man: his face was like a punctured, empty bubble that had collapsed into folds, with something transparent still leaking out of the puncture and trickling slowly down. Gradually,

241

dimly, I realised that the something was tears. Only when the man was well past me did I recollect myself and call him.

"Listen, listen, you don't know Number I-330, do you?..."

The old man looked round, gestured despairingly and hobbled on...

I returned home at dusk. The western sky was being racked every few moments by a pale-blue convulsion, there was a hollow, muffled din coming from that direction. The roofs were dotted with burnt-out black embers: birds.

I lay down on my bed and straightaway sleep, like a wild beast, overcame me, suffocating me under its body...

Entry No. 38

Summary:

(I DON'T KNOW
WHAT IT SHOULD BE:
PERHAPS THE WHOLE SUMMARY
IS SIMPLY "THE DISCARDED
CIGARETTE")

When I came to, it was bright daylight and painful to look at. I screwed up my eyes. There was a kind of acrid, dark-blue mist in my head, everything was shrouded in fog. And through the fog:

"But I haven't put the light on, after all—so how..."

I jumped up. Seated at the table, her chin propped up on her hand, I-330 was regarding me with amusement...

I am writing at that very table now. Those ten or fifteen minutes are already past, cruelly coiled up into a very tight spring. But it seems to me that the door has only just closed behind her and I could still overtake her, seize her by the hands and, perhaps, she would laugh and say...

She was sitting at the table. I rushed towards her.

"It's you, it's you! I've been—I saw your room, I thought you—"

But halfway there I ran into sharp, motionless spears of eyelashes and stopped. I remembered how she had looked at me just like that on board *Integral*. But I must now, immediately, in a single second, manage to tell her so that she would believe me, otherwise never, never again...

"Listen, I must... I must tell you everything... No, no, I'll just—I'll just have a drink of water..."

My mouth was dry, as if lined with blotting-paper. I poured out some water, but I couldn't drink it. I put the tumbler on the table and gripped the carafe firmly with both hands.

I now saw that the blue mist was from a cigarette. She raised it to her lips, drew in, greedily swallowed the smoke, just as I had tried to gulp down the water, and said:

"Don't. Be quiet. It makes no difference. You

can see I've come anyway. They're waiting for me downstairs. And you want our last minutes together..."

She threw the cigarette on to the floor, stretched her whole body back over the arm of her chair (it was hard for her to reach the switch in the wall from where she was sitting) and I remembered how the chair rocked and its two legs detached themselves from the floor. Then the blinds came down.

She came up and hugged me tight. Her knees through the dress—a slow, gentle, warm, all-enveloping poison...

And suddenly... These things happen: you're wholly immersed in a sweet, warm dream, when suddenly something stings you, you tremble and your eyes are wide open again... So it was this time: trampled rose-red tickets scattered all over the floor of her room, and on one of them the letter F and some numbers... They clustered into a ball inside me, and even now I can't describe my feelings, but I gripped her so hard that she cried out with pain...

Yet one more minute out of those ten or fifteen, on the brilliant white pillow— her head thrown back with her eyes half-closed; the sharp, sweet stripe of the teeth. And all the time it was insistently, incongruously and agonisingly reminding me of something that is forbidden, of what I mustn't mention now. And I hugged her more and more tenderly, more and more cruelly, and the dark blue marks from my fingers were becoming more and more vivid...

She said (without, I noticed, opening her eyes), "They say you were with the Benefactor yesterday. Is that true?"

"Yes, it is."

Then her eyes opened wide, and I watched with pleasure as her face quickly turned pale, was obliterated, disappeared: nothing left but the eyes.

I told her everything. And only—I don't know why ... no, that's not true, I do know—only about one thing did I keep quiet: about what He had said at the very end, about my being necessary to them only...

Gradually, like a photographic print in the developer, her face emerged: cheeks, the white strip of the teeth, lips. She stood up and went to the mirror-door of the wardrobe.

Dryness in the mouth again. I poured myself out some water, but it tasted revolting. I put the tumbler on the table and asked:

"Is that why you came—because you needed to find out?"

She looked at me from the mirror—a sharp, mocking triangle of eyebrows tilted upwards towards the temples. She glanced round to say something to me, but did not do so.

There was no need. I knew.

Say goodbye to her? I moved my—someone else's—legs and accidentally caught the chair so that it fell on to its back, as dead as back there in her room. Her lips were cold, as the floor by my bed here in this room had once been cold.

When she went out, I sat down on the floor and bent over the cigarette she had discarded.

I can't write any more. I don't want to!

Entry No. 39
Summary:
THE END.

All this was like the last grain of salt thrown into a saturated solution: quickly, becoming spiky with needles, the crystals began to crawl, solidified and set. It was clear to me that everything was decided and tomorrow morning I would do it. It would be like killing myself, but only then, perhaps, would I be resurrected. For only the dead can be resurrected.

In the west, the sky was shuddering every second in a dark-blue convulsion. My head was burning and throbbing. I sat like that all night and only fell asleep at about seven o'clock in the morning when the darkness had already withdrawn into itself, and the roofs, dotted with birds, were now visible...

I woke up. It was already ten (there had evidently been no bell that day). Yesterday's tumbler of water was still standing on the table. I greedily gulped it down and rushed out: I had to get it all done as soon as possible.

The sky was desolate and pale-blue, scoured clean by the storm. The prickly angles of shadows, everything carved out of blue autumnal air and so delicate that it would be terrible to touch: it would immediately crack, disintegrate into glass dust. And it was the same within me; I daren't think, I mustn't think, otherwise— —

Indeed, I wasn't thinking, perhaps I wasn't even seeing properly, I was simply registering. Over there on the roadway were branches from somewhere; their leaves were green, amber, mulberry-red. Overhead, birds and aeros were criss-crossing as they darted to and fro. I could see heads, open mouths, hands waving branches. All that must have been roaring, croaking, buzzing...

Then the streets, as empty as if swept clean by some kind of pestilence. I remember stumbling over something unbearably soft, yielding and yet immo-veable. I bent down. It was a corpse. It was lying on its back with its knees up and parted, like those of a woman. Its face...

I recognised the fat, negroid and, even now, laughter-spluttering lips. His eyes closed tight, he was laughing into my face. A second later I stepped over him and fled because I couldn't bear it any longer, I must do everything as quickly as possible, otherwise, I felt, I would break or bend like an over-loaded rail...

Fortunately, within twenty paces there was a notice in gold lettering: "Guardians' Bureau". I stopped on the threshold, sipped as much air as I could and went in.

Inside, in the corridor, there was an endless file of numbers all holding sheets of paper or thick notebooks in their hands. They were moving forward a pace or two at a time, then stopping again.

I began rushing up and down alongside the file, my head bobbing this way and that. I clutched them by the sleeves, I implored them as a sick man begs for something that will put an agonising but mercifully quick end to his dreadful suffering.

There was a woman, her waist tightly bound round with a belt over her unifa. The two hemispheres of her buttocks were bulgingly prominent, and she kept swinging them from side to side, as if that was where her eyes were.

"He's got stomach-ache!" she whinnied at me. "Take him to the toilet—over there, second door on the right..."

I was overcome by laughter. And that laughter made something rise to my throat, and I was going to scream at any moment or... or...

Suddenly, someone gripped me by the elbow from behind. I looked round: transparent, winged ears. Except that they were not rosy, as usual, but leaden-hued. His Adam's apple was twitching—it would burst through the thin covering at any moment.

"What are you doing here?" he asked, his eyes drilling fast into me.

I latched desperately on to him.

"Quick, to your office... I must... everything. Now! It's a good thing that its to you of all peo-

248

ple... Perhaps it's appalling, but it's a good thing, it's a good thing..."

He also knew her and this made it even more agonising for me but, perhaps, he too would shudder when he heard, and we would kill together; I would not be alone at my last moment...

The door slammed. I remember that a paper stuck to the underneath of the door and scraped over the floor when the door was closing, and then a special, airless silence came down like a hood. If he had said a single thing, never mind what, never mind how trivial, I would have started everything straightaway, but he did not speak.

So tense that my ears began buzzing, I said, without looking at him:

"I think I must always have hated her, right from the start. I fought it... But no, no, don't believe me: I could have escaped and didn't want to, I wanted to perish, that meant more to me than anything ... that is, not to perish, but to make her... And even now, even now, when I know everything... Do you know that the Benefactor sent for me?"

"Yes, I do."

"But what He said to me... Please understand, it would be just like snatching the rug from under your feet, and you with everything on that table—paper, ink ... the ink would spill over and everything would be blotted out..."

"Go on, go on! And hurry up. Others are waiting out there."

And then, choking, confused, I told him everything that's written in this diary. About myself real and myself shaggy, and what she said about my hands—yes, that was where it all began—and how I didn't want to carry out my duty at the time, and how I deceived myself, and how she got hold of false certificates, and how I went to seed from day to day, and the corridors down below, and how over there, on the other side of the Wall...

I stammered all this out in incoherent gobbets and scraps—haltingly—I couldn't find the words. The curved, double-bent lips smilingly prompted me with the words I needed, and I nodded gratefully: yes, yes... And now—what was the meaning of this?—he was speaking for me, and I was only listening: "Yes, and then... That's just how it was, yes, yes!"

I felt a coldness beginning to come right round my collar, as from the ether, and I asked with an effort:

"But how?... But there's nowhere you could have got that from..."

His smile, in silence, was becoming more and more twisted... And then:

"But, you know, you wanted to hide something from me, you counted up all those you noticed beyond the wall, but missed one of them. You say no? But don't you remember that fleetingly, for a fraction of a second there, you saw—me? Yes, yes, me."

Pause.

And suddenly, in a flash, right to the head, it became shamelessly clear: he was one of them too... And all of me, all my torments, everything that I had brought here at my last gasp as an act of heroism was merely ridiculous, it was like the ancient jest about Abraham and Isaac. Abraham, in a cold sweat, had already raised the knife over his son, over himself, when suddenly there came a voice from on high: "It's not worth it! I was joking..."

Not taking my eyes off the smile that was becoming more and more twisted, I leaned my arms on the edge of the table, slowly, very slowly slid back with the armchair, then suddenly pulled myself together and raced headlong past shouts, stairs, open mouths...

I don't remember how I ended up down below in one of the public toilets at the underground station. Up above, on the surface, everything was perishing, the greatest and most rational of all human civilisations in history was crashing to the ground, but here, by some irony, everything was as before, beautiful. And to think that all this was doomed, all this would be overgrown with grass and nothing would be left of it all but "myths".

I groaned loudly. And at that moment I felt someone affectionately stroking my shoulder.

It was my neighbour, sitting on my left. His brow was an enormous bald parabola, there were the yellow, indecipherable lines of wrinkles on his forehead. And those lines were about me.

"I understand you, I understand you completely," he said. "But calm down, nevertheless. Don't behave like that. It will all come back, it will irretrievably all come back. The only important thing is that all should know about my discovery. You are the first to hear of this. I have worked out by calculation that there is no such thing as infinity!"

I looked wildly at him.

"Yes, yes, I'm telling you there is no such thing as infinity. If the world is infinite, then the average density of the matter in it must be equal to zero. But since it is not zero—we know this—then, consequently the Universe's radius, $y2$ = the average density multiplied by... That's all I need—to calculate the numerical coefficient, and then... Everything is finite, you understand, everything is elementary, everything is calculable; and then we shall win philosophically, d'you understand? And you, my esteemed friend, are preventing me from finishing my calculations; you are shouting..."

I don't know which shook me more: his discovery or his toughness at that apocalyptic hour. He was holding (I now noticed it for the first time) a notebook and a logarithmic dial in his hands. And I realised that even if everything perished, my duty (before you, my dear unknown readers) was to leave my notes in finished form.

I asked him for some paper and there and then I wrote down these last lines...

I was just about to put in the last full-stop, the way the ancients set up a cross over the pits in which they had thrown the dead, but suddenly the pencil began trembling and fell from my fingers...

"Listen," I said, clutching at my neighbour, "you've got to listen to me! You must, must answer! What about where your finite Universe ends? What's out there beyond it?"

He didn't get the chance to reply: the tramp of feet coming down the stairs from up above— —

Entry No. 40
Summary:

FACTS. THE BELL. I AM CERTAIN.

Daytime. Clear. Barometer 760.

Did I, D-503, really write these two hundred and twenty pages? Did I really once feel all this, or imagine that I felt it?

The handwriting is mine. It's the same further on but, fortunately, only the handwriting. No crazy thoughts, no incongruous metaphors, no feelings: just facts. Because I am fit, I am completely, absolutely fit. I smile, because I cannot help smiling. They've pulled a kind of splinter out of my brain and my head is now light and empty. To be more precise, not empty, but there is nothing extraneous, nothing that prevents me from smiling (a smile is the normal condition of the normal human being).

The facts are these. That evening, my neighbour, who had discovered the finiteness of the Universe, and I myself, and all who were with us at the time, were taken to the nearest auditorium (its number, 112, is familiar for some reason). We were tied down to tables in there and subjected to the Great Operation.

On the next day, I, D-503, reported to the Benefactor and told him everything known to me about the enemies of happiness. Why could this have seemed so difficult to me before? I don't understand. The only explanation can be my former illness (soul).

In the evening of the same day, at the same table with Him, the Benefactor, I was sitting (for the first time) in the famous Gas Room. They brought her in, that woman. She was to give her testimony in my presence. She was stubbornly silent and kept smiling. I noticed that she had sharp, very white teeth, and that this was beautiful.

She was then taken under the Bell. Her face became very white, and since her eyes were dark and big, this was very beautiful. When they began pumping the air out of the Bell, she threw back her head, half-closed her eyes and clenched her teeth. It reminded me of something. She stared and stared at me, tightly clutching the arms of her chair until her eyes were fully closed. Then she was quickly pulled out, revived with electrodes and again made to sit in the chair under the Bell. This was repeated three times, and yet she never said a word. Others, who had been brought with that woman, proved more honest. Many of them started talking straightaway. Tomorrow they will all climb the stairway to the Benefactor's Machine.

There must be no delay, because there are still

bodies, beasts, howling and chaos in the western quarters and, unfortunately, a great many numbers who have lost their reason.

But a temporary Wall of high-tension waves has successfully been erected on the transverse 40th Prospekt. And I hope that we shall triumph. More than that, I am certain that we shall triumph. Because reason itself must triumph.

Евгений Замятин

Мы

Подробнее ознакомиться с содержанием
и оформлением наших книг можно по Интернету.
Наш адрес: **www.raduga.express.ru**

ИБ № 8903

Редакторы *Н. Вергелис, О. Чоракаев*
Оформление *А. Никулина*
Художественный редактор *Т. Иващенко*
Технический редактор *Е. Макарова*

Сдано в набор 20.09.99. Подписано в печать 08.10.99.
Формат 70 × 100/32. Бумага офсетная. Гарнитура Таймс.
Печать офсетная. Условн. печ. л. 10,32. Уч.-изд. л. 9,44.
Тираж 5 000 экз. Заказ № 1578. Изд. № 8903.

Налоговая льгота — общероссийский классификатор
продукции ОК-005-93, том 2;
953000 — книги, брошюры.

Лицензия ЛР № 020846 от 23 декабря 1998 г.
ОАО Издательство «Радуга»
121839, Москва, пер. Сивцев Вражек, 43.

Отпечатано способом фотоофсет
в ОАО «Можайский полиграфический комбинат»
143200, Можайск, ул. Мира, 93.